MISSING PIECES

BY CARLY ANNE WEST

ART BY TIM HEITZ

Scholastic Inc.

Library of Congress Cataloging-in-Publication Data available

ISBN 978-1-338-28007-4

10 9 8 7 6 5 4 3 2 1 18 19 20 21 22
Printed in the U.S.A. 23
First printing 2018

Book design by Cheung Tai

PROLOGUE

That isn't dreaming, my grandma used to say. *That's your soul getting into trouble.*

I was what my parents called a restless sleeper. My grandma knew better, though. It's like she was there when I closed my eyes and drifted off. When I would wake up, she'd make me wash my hands, just like she did, first thing every morning.

She'd click her tongue while she scrubbed my hands raw, shaking off the water and raking them dry with a towel.

You're the wandering type, she'd say sometimes. *Your soul makes your body wander, makes you get lost*. Then she would watch me closely as I ran off to my room to get dressed for the day. Even after I closed the door, I could hear her scolding me: *You stop that wandering, Boychik! Or one day, you won't make it home!*

That's when my dreams turned to nightmares.

My grandma was nearly blind when she died, but she saw me clearer than anyone ever has.

Until I met Aaron.

CHAPTER 1

"Nicholas, now means *now*!" Mom yells from the foot of the stairs. With the house empty, her voice bounces toward me like a ball, careening off the walls and straight through my aching head.

"Give him another minute, Lu." Dad's voice is quieter, but the sound of it still hurts. I know they think I was up all night doing something I wasn't supposed to be doing like playing video games and eating Cheez Whiz from the can, but I was actually up all night doing nothing at all. I was staring at the wall, then staring at the ceiling, then staring at the fly that got stuck on the tail end of the packing tape that came loose from the box holding my tools and three dismantled CB radios.

"We're paying the movers by the hour, Jay. Either he comes now or the new tenants are going to have to adopt him."

"Time to go, Narf," Dad says as I trudge downstairs, and I smile because Dad's trying. In her own way, I think Mom's trying, too.

"Yikes," Dad says after Mom kisses me a little too hard on the head and walks out the door.

"What?"

"That smile is fooling no one. It looks creepy," he says.

I stop, and now we can both relax.

"I know this is bad," he says, rubbing the back of his head. "Devastatingly bad."

"It's just a few states over," I say, repeating what Mom has said every day for the past three months.

"That's light-years away," says Dad, and thank the Giant Space Alien Overlords that someone is finally telling the truth.

"Yeah, my legions of friends begged me not to go. They made me promise I'd write," I say, and the smile slips from Dad's face because he knows I'm faking it again.

"This just wasn't your city," he says. "Raven Brooks, though, Raven Brooks will be your city."

He closes the door to the house that never really felt like my house, just like the last one didn't and the one before that.

"Goodbye, Red House," Mom says as she eyes it in the rearview mirror, following the moving truck a little too closely down the long driveway. She gets teary-eyed, and Dad gives her shoulder a little squeeze.

"Raven Brooks will be our city," he says again, this time so Mom can hear it, and she looks about as convinced as I feel. We drive 715 miles in near silence, swallowing the lie that Raven Brooks really isn't that far from Charleston, just like we swallowed the lie that the blue house in Ontario was any different from the brown house in Oakland or the yellow house in Redding or the beige house in Coeur d'Alene. The lies get a little bigger with each move—with each realization that towns don't need newspaper editors if they don't have newspapers to edit anymore, but landlords still need rent money no matter what.

So what was one more move, one more town, one more new school and new house that wouldn't really be our house anyway? I only had to get used to it for a little while. This time, maybe I wouldn't even unpack.

CHAPTER 2

The new house is turquoise.

"I'd call it more of a . . . blue-green," Mom says, tilting her head like maybe that would change the color.

"Teal," Dad offers. "It used to be a very popular color for exteriors."

Dad knows nothing about exteriors, or colors for that matter. That's the thing about newspaper editors, though. They can sound like experts on just about anything.

"Wasn't it white in the pictures?" Mom asks.

The moving truck rumbles up the otherwise quiet street called—I swear to the Aliens—Friendly Court, then the driver leans out the window.

"This one yours? The turquoise one?"

Mom drops her head. "I give up."

Dad nods to the driver. "The turquoise one."

The truck reverses and backs into the driveway, and just like that, we're Jay, Luanne, and Nicky Roth, of 909 Friendly Court, Raven Brooks. This fall I'll be an eighth grader at Raven Brooks Middle School, where I'll excel in science and English and struggle in math and Spanish. I'll be that short kid in the Beatles T-shirt, whom everyone mistakenly calls "Nate," with the brown hair that sticks up on the left side no matter how much water I use to flatten it. I'll eat Jell-O pudding packs every day and clear the lunch table because there's no reason why I shouldn't, and I'll spend the rest of the lunch period taking things apart and putting them back together.

"It's a nice street," Dad says of the mostly pristine lawns and neatly shuttered windows. The paint is a little faded, the cars are a little old, but we've lived on worse blocks, and I even see a cat or two crouched in flower beds across the street. Cats feel like a good sign.

"It's quiet," Mom says, and it's hard to tell if that's praise or worry in her voice.

"There's a llama farm," I say, and my parents look at me. "I saw a sign," I explain, and then we're quiet again.

"Well," Dad says after a while, "I think I've earned a Ho Ho."

Mom's always complaining that Dad never lost his childhood sweet tooth, but there's a grown-up method to his sugar madness. Once you figure out the pattern, it's pretty easy to tell how Dad's feeling. Ho Hos mean he's exhausted. Ding Dongs are the treat of choice for when he's happy. Pounding down Suzy Q's? It's time to celebrate! But the real telltale cakes are the yellow ones. Zingers can

mean only one thing—Dad's sad. Twinkies are for when he's pondering life's big questions—big Alien-Overlord-in-the-Sky questions.

Mom sighs. "Jay, you've had three already."

"What's that, dear? I can't hear you. It's Ho Ho'clock!"

I start to follow them into the house but decide to take in the quiet of the street a little bit longer. Maybe if I hang out long enough, one of the cats will come over. I take a seat on the curb in front of our new turquoise house and pull the long blades of grass that shoot up on either side of me. I'm lost in thoughts of my latest project—a knot of old padlocks I found in an empty lot by the red house. Five different padlocks, all interlocked with no keys. I've managed to pick two of them, but the other three are giving me trouble. Locks are my new project, specifically lock*picking*. It feels like I'm taking something apart without actually deconstructing it, like I'm discovering the secret from the inside out. I tried to explain it to Mom once, but I don't think she understood; she's more into stuff you can see under a microscope.

"I think you're amazing, Nicky," she'd said, then tilted my chin up to meet her stern gaze. "Just use your powers for good."

That's the warning she attaches to pretty much everything I do, a reminder that even the smartest people can make dumb decisions.

Movement from across the street breaks my trance, and at first I think it's one of the cats, but I don't see them anymore. All I see is a curtain billow on the second story of the house across the street. I stare harder, but I can't see whoever moved the curtain. All I see is the reflection of a twisted oak tree that practically touches the window, it looms so close. Someone was watching me, though. That's a feeling you just know, like when the air smells different before a storm. I watch the window for a little bit longer until I get sick of waiting.

"Stare at me all you want," I tell the empty window. "Nothing to see here."

I stand to go inside, already folding on my decision not to unpack. *Maybe just the box with the padlocks*, I think. Then I hear a tiny mewing sound behind me—one of those all-gray cats with blue eyes. He looks like he's been rolling in campfire ash all night. Even his whiskers look dusty. He winds his body around my leg, making a figure eight and circling my other ankle. On his side is a greasy black streak, like he's been sidling up to a newly waxed car tire.

"Hey, cat," I say. I've never been great with names.

He mews in response.

"You live across the street?"

Another mew.

"Well, tell Creeper up there that it's not polite to stare."

I reach for his head to scratch behind his ears, but then he locks eyes with me, and something changes. The fur on his tail and spine stand on end, and his ears fall back against his skull. Eyes wide, he's suddenly a different cat. A quick hiss and a swipe, and my new friend leaves a long, fine scratch along my hand and wrist.

Yanking my hand away, I'm about to shoo him off when I see him staring up at the window across the street, and this time, the curtain is pulled back. A face—I think it's a face—hovers at the edge of the frame, not exactly hiding, but not front and center, either. Maybe it's the glare of the sun off the glass, but the face is so white, I'm nearly positive it's just a light fixture or something I'm seeing. But no, those are eyes and a nose . . .

The cat hisses again, still staring at the window. Then his fur lowers, his ears pull forward, and he stands from his crouch, returning his focus to me. I look back at the window and see the same billowing curtain as before. No face, no glare. Just fabric behind glass.

"I don't think you and I are going to be friends," I say to the cat, or maybe to the face in the window. Either way, the cat slinks across the street to his flower bed, and I retreat to my new house to see which locks are easiest to pick.

* * *

I wake up and forget where I am for a minute, one of my least favorite things about moving. The room doesn't smell like mine yet; in Charleston, it smelled like a mix of salted meat and vanilla air freshener. Here, it smells the way the main library in Coeur d'Alene smelled, like old wood and a little bit of mold.

My sheets are soaked with sweat, and I dig a new shirt out of an open box before giving up on sleep for the rest of the night. Not a chance I'll be able to shake that nightmare; I never can. I was in the grocery store again, sitting in the shopping cart, my feet dangling high above the floor. It was cold and dark, and the shelves of canned foods towered so high above me, I was afraid they were going to fall and crush me. Like always, I wanted to get out of the cart, to find help or find out where I was. Like always, I was afraid to move.

It's weird—in the dream, I'm frozen. In real life, I would give anything for my family to stay in one place for once. Then I remember that the scariest place my dreams take me is to the grocery store, and I decide that I probably shouldn't try to make too much sense out of them.

I drag my locks to the deep windowsill that faces the street. It's the coolest part of my new room, this built-in bench that creates the perfect spot to sit and stare out at the rest of Friendly Court. I can see all the way to the highway if I face the right direction. For now, though, all I see is the house across the street, which is fine because I know I'm the only one up at . . .

I turn my watch over on my desk.

"Three fifteen."

I press my hand over my eyes and cup my forehead, massaging my temples. It's going to be a long day.

I unearth my pick set and get to work on the lock that's been giving me the most trouble.

With my flashlight, I try to see as far into the hole as I can, but it's a classic shrouded shackle, and I can see only so far. I've been using the torsion wrench to hold the plug in place, but the half-diamond pick is too rigid to make it very far through those angles.

"Ball pick," I say under my breath, rummaging through the worn leather case of tools I bought from some kid just outside of Charleston who seemed a little too eager to get rid of it.

"There you are," I say to the titanium alloy stick with the circle tip.

I start to work the pick through the lock and make it around one corner, then another, until the pin starts to lift.

"Almost there," I say, the familiar rush of besting the lock beginning to wash over me. Maybe this day won't be so bad after all.

Then a scream cuts through the night air.

I drop the knot of locks on the floor, and the crash echoes through the house, but I'm not focused on that. I'm straining to hear the last echoes of the scream that should have woken the entire neighborhood. Not a single light on the street flickers, though. Not one head pops out their front door to see what's going on.

The voice was high and ragged, and at first it sounded like a kid, but then I'm not so sure. I've heard some pretty convincing goats make that screaming sound, and there *was* that llama farm we saw on the way into town . . .

I hold so still, I forget to blink, and my eyes water until I rub them. When my vision clears, I'm staring once again at the window on the second story of the house across the street. This time, I'm sure I see a face staring back at me.

"You again," I whisper, and I half expect to hear an answer. Instead, the head moves closer to the window, eventually pressing against the pane. Hands cup around the face, like binoculars, and I do the same. I'm staring at a boy who looks my age. It might be the glare of moonlight or the contrast against the night sky, but the kid's hair looks almost white, like he got struck by lightning in an old sci-fi movie.

We stand there, hands shielding our faces, staring for a strangely long time, and just when I'm starting to get a little uncomfortable with this game of chicken, he slaps his hand against the window, a yellow sheet of notebook paper glowing in front of the circular light of a flashlight.

He heard me talking to the cat.

I take my hand from the window and back up a little, looking for the string to pull the shade. Before I find it, though, the kid drops the note and flickers his light to get my attention. Then he slaps another note to the window.

Then he smiles.

I look down at my kit and the knot of locks, feeling found out, but instead of being embarrassed, I feel . . . relieved.

I rummage for a piece of paper and a marker we'd been using to label boxes. I think for a second, then hold my flashlight up to my own message.

The kid smiles, and he ducks his head, showing me a full head of lightning-white hair, then holds up a new sheet.

I nod, and he draws his curtain closed, leaving me standing there with my flashlight in one hand and a marker in the other. I stare at the house across the street, which is definitely bigger than ours but I'm not sure I'd call it nicer. From the chipped paint on the porch to the cracked driveway to the gutters separating at the seams, everything looks like it's in need of repair. Upon closer look, there's a little half door on the side of the house that looks like it might lead to a root cellar, but it's impossible to say because if it is a door, it's covered over with so many wooden boards and bent nails, there's no way it could ever open. If that weren't enough, metal padlocks gleam from hinges between the wooden boards, daring someone to try to gain entry. Overkill doesn't even begin to cover it.

I shake my head and go back to bed, staring up at the ceiling, the sound of my dad's words swirling around in my brain.

Raven Brooks will be your city.

Maybe it will be. There's the windowsill like a bench and a kid across the street who knows the difference between a half-diamond and a ball pick. There's a newspaper that everyone still subscribes to, and a university where Mom's giant science brain is needed.

I'm almost asleep again before I remember why I was looking out the window in the first place. I settle into an uneasy sleep with the memory of a scream that no one but me seemed to hear.

CHAPTER 3

The kid across the street is named Aaron Peterson, and his house is made of doors. Not really, but it feels that way. The first time I go over, I open three doors before I finally find the bathroom. Then I go to the kitchen for a glass of water and get lost trying to find his room.

"Don't feel bad. Everyone gets a little turned around at first," he tells me after I finally find my way back. Then he shrugs. "Old houses are weird."

I nod like I agree, but I've lived in old houses. The turquoise house is old, too. None of them have been like this one, though, with side staircases that lead to little half landings, and some doors that don't even open.

When I was seven, we lived in Northern California for a few months while my dad was still a beat reporter. My mom, always up for a good ghost story, took me to the Winchester mansion, where we got to tour the house that was perpetually, obsessively built by the widow of the famous Winchester rifle maker. The story went that someone told her she and her family were being haunted by the thousands of people who'd lost their lives to her husband's gun company. She kept the builders working day and night on a house she would never finish building so the ghosts couldn't find her in the maze of a mansion. The clearest memory I took away from the tour was a door that opened to a three-story drop. I imagined a sleepy seven-year-old me staying in that twisty house, waking in the middle of the night looking for someplace to pee and dropping to my death after pulling the wrong knob.

"We don't have one of those," Aaron tells me when I relay my memory to him the next day. "At least I don't think we do."

He says it so casually, I don't think he realizes how strange it is that he could live in a house and not know where every door leads. At least, at first it seems strange to me. Then I learn that there are some places in Aaron's house that are off-limits.

"The basement's kind of a wreck," he says, but now he's less casual about it. Now he seems uncomfortable. I think back on the boarded-up door on the side of their house, the one I thought led to a root cellar.

Aaron doesn't have white hair, as it turns out. That was a trick of the flashlight, just one of the many weird aspects of the night he introduced himself to me. It's just light brown, but that's about the only ordinary quality about Aaron. He's tall—in fact, at first I thought maybe he was older than me. He's my age, though, and he acts like he's fifty. It's like the Giant Alien Overlords sucked all the childhood out of him and left behind a twelve-year-old adult. It's not that he doesn't smile or joke. He just has . . . purpose.

He's also better at picking locks than me. He can find his way into the tiniest keyhole, his hands steady and precise. But that isn't why he's good. It's his patience that makes him better than me. He can sit in a turn and twitch the pick a millimeter, feel for the movement, then guide the tool through a different path, until *boom!* The lock springs free, and the door opens.

"I should've gone with the rake," I say, angry at myself

for not springing the hall closet upstairs that particular afternoon.

"I'll give you an easier one next time," he says, punching my shoulder a little too hard.

I punch him back harder. "Man, don't be a—"

"A what?"

Broad shoulders and an argyle sweater emerge from a door behind us that I swear to the Aliens I didn't even know was a door.

"Uh . . ."

"Dad, this is Nicky. From across the street."

"Nicky from across the street," Mr. Peterson says, pinching an end of his curled mustache like a cartoon villain. And he looks like he could be a villain, with his wide eyes hooded by thick eyebrows and forearms bigger than my legs. If not for his unmistakable dad uniform—violet-blue sweater, brown pants, high socks—I'd be halfway across the street by now.

He didn't ask me a question, but he's looking at me like he's waiting on an answer.

"Uh, we were just . . ."

Picking locks in your house.

Fighting.

Cursing.

Mr. Peterson leans over and puts his hands on his knees, large shoulders framing the face that's now six inches from mine. His carnival mustache is practically touching my cheek. I can smell spearmint on his breath.

"Well, Nicky from across the street," he says, and I clench my teeth together to keep them from chattering.

He leans in even closer, and I think I'm going to faint.

"How would you like . . . to stay for dinner?"

He pauses and waits for me to process what wasn't the threat it sounded like, and then his mustache lifts to reveal a row of brilliant white teeth. He leans back, tilts his head, and bellows a laugh that shakes the hallway I nearly pee myself in.

I start to laugh, too, because I have no idea what else to do. I feel Aaron grab my arm and drag me down the stairs, muttering something about "Don't know why you have to be so weird" and shoves me down the hallway so I can gather myself and wonder if he was calling his dad weird or me.

I start to head down a different hallway before Aaron redirects me. Just one more rabbit hole to fall through in his winding house.

In the kitchen, Aaron's ten-year-old sister is wielding a seriously sharp knife over a yellow onion while Mrs. Peterson smokes a cigarette with her back turned. Aaron told me his mom teaches first grade at Raven Brooks Elementary.

"Cripes, Mya, give me that." Aaron lunges toward the

cutting board and catches the handle of the knife just as Mya begins to pierce the wobbly onion against the wood.

"Mom asked me to," she says defensively, but she looks relieved.

"You know I'm a crier," Mrs. Peterson says, exhaling a stream of smoke through the kitchen window screen.

"I have freakishly strong eyes," Mya says, her pride returning after being stripped of her duties. She's Aaron's polar opposite, with light red hair like her mother's. She shares her mother's small frame, too, with stubby little legs that make her look younger than she should.

Aaron slices the onion into fine rings and sets the knife and cutting board in the middle of the kitchen island while Mya wipes the onion skin from where it got caught on her watch.

"Thanks, baby," Mrs. Peterson says, stubbing out her cigarette and planting a kiss on top of Aaron's head, then one on my head, and I turn away when my face gets hot, and for some reason, Mya's face gets red, too. Mrs. Peterson lets me call her Diane, but it feels so weird I've just stopped calling her anything at all. I guess she's pretty, but she reminds me so much of my mom it's nuts.

I've tried to get Mom to invite the Petersons over for dinner, but Mom's formal about stuff like that. "They should invite us first," Mom says, and that's that.

"Hamburgers for dinner tonight," Mrs. Peterson says.

"You boys planning on sticking around, or are you robbing banks this evening?"

I turn to face the wall again because I had a dream last night that I cracked a bank vault, and the rush I felt was so strong I felt a little awkward when I woke up. I'm pretty sure that's not using my powers for good.

"Who's robbing banks?" Mr. Peterson says, emerging once again from whatever kind of shadow a hulking guy in argyle can hide in.

"Oh," Mrs. Peterson says, peering into her mixing bowl. "We might not have enough hamburger if you stay, Nicky. Aaron, you'd have to run to the store for some more."

"Batty Mrs. Tillman stopped selling meat, remember?" Aaron says.

"Oh, that's right. I keep forgetting that," says Mrs. Peterson.

Aaron turns to me with a wicked smile. "We could get you a tasty bulgur-wheat-and-tofu burger, though. Maybe a cocoa-powder granola bar for dessert."

"Whatever, you love those bars," Mya says, curling her lip.

"It's true," Aaron says, leaning toward me. "They make you fart."

Mya dissolves into giggles.

"A *lot*."

"What's the verdict on dinner?" Mrs. Peterson asks, bringing us back on topic. "You boys in or out?"

"We're eating at Nicky's," Aaron says, and when I look at him, he widens his eyes.

"Right. At my house," I say, not much better at lying than Aaron is.

Mrs. Peterson examines us from across the kitchen island. Mya swoops in to save the day, though, bringing us back to a forgotten topic.

"Everyone thinks that Jesse James was the best bank robber there was, just because he was a show-off, but he couldn't have done any of that without his brother, Frank. People always forget the siblings."

"I'm sure you could rob a bank just as successfully as your brother, Mouse," Mrs. Peterson says, lining the patties into perfect rows on the cutting board. She holds a meat tenderizer high above her head and brings it down with startling strength, moving from patty to patty with unsettling enthusiasm.

Mya rolls her eyes, but I can tell she likes when her mom calls her Mouse, just like I don't mind that my dad still calls me Narf. My parents claim that's how I used to say my name before I could say Nick, which is weird because it doesn't even sound the same, but whatever. It stuck, so now I'm Narf, and from some of the nicknames I've heard out there, it could be a whole lot worse.

"And I'm sure your brother wouldn't dream of taking credit for your accomplishments," Mrs. Peterson adds, winking at Aaron.

She brings the meat hammer down on the patty again, and I jump before I can catch myself.

"Remember, family makes you stronger," Mrs. Peterson says. "Isn't that right, honey?"

Mrs. Peterson turns her head to the side to address her husband, but her eyes never meet his. Mr. Peterson just stands there for a second, surveying his family across the kitchen island before moving to the sink to wash his hands.

"Not necessarily," he says with his back turned to us all, and from the way he says it, I can tell that's all he wants to say on the subject.

Either Mrs. Peterson doesn't notice or she doesn't care. "Oh, don't be a grump. You don't really mean that."

Mrs. Peterson flashes me a smile and rolls her eyes, which might be convincing if her hands weren't shaking so hard she has to set down the meat tenderizer.

Mr. Peterson scrubs his fingernails meticulously at the sink. I sneak a glance at Aaron, and he's watching his dad, too. Mya's moved to the other side of the island, and she's fidgeting with the ties on one of the barstool cushions. I'm waiting for the punch line, for Mr. Peterson to whip around and bark that insane laugh from under his mustache, but he doesn't turn around.

Mrs. Peterson tries a joke. "Well, I'm afraid you're stuck with us, darling. We're Petersons to the bone."

Now Mr. Peterson does turn around, so fast that the towel in his hands makes a whipping sound in the air.

"You know what's so interesting about bones, Diane?" he says with a smile that's way different than the one he cracked in the hallway upstairs. This one bares both rows of his teeth, and they don't part. He just talks right through them.

Mya moves a little closer to Aaron. I think I do, too.

"Not all of them are necessary."

Mya reaches for Aaron's hand, and he squeezes hers back.

"It's true," Mr. Peterson continues, even though no one contested it. "It's remarkable what the human body can survive without. Pluck one bone out, and the body keeps on living."

Mrs. Peterson is shaping the hamburger patties, and she's been working on that same patty since her husband started talking; I don't think she's thinking about hamburgers anymore. She closes her eyes, and I want to close mine, too, but I'm afraid to look away.

"There's just one bone you can't live without . . . the funny bone!"

Mr. Peterson runs to Mya and scoops her up by the waist, and for a panicked second, I think he's actually going to hurt her. But she starts giggling immediately, and her giggle turns to a frantic laugh, and I see that he's not hurting her at all; he's tickling her ribs.

"Where's that bone? Where's that funny bone?" he says, suddenly playful, and I think I misconstrued the whole scene, until I look at Aaron and Mrs. Peterson, who are sharing a look I can't quite understand. It's solemn, though, nothing like the exchange Mr. Peterson is having with Mya as he throws her over his shoulder and begins to spin her around.

"Let's go," Aaron says to me under his breath, and I don't argue.

Once we're outside, we don't say a word until we're at least three blocks from our street and halfway to the train tracks on the other side of the woods that border Raven Brooks. The rain from earlier has stopped, but the ground still squishes when we walk.

"Where're we going?" I ask Aaron when I feel like it's okay to ask him anything at all.

"You'll see," he says, but doesn't look at me. "There's something I want to show you."

CHAPTER 4

The factory should be fenced off. Maybe it was at some point, but it sure isn't now. And we shouldn't be able to walk right through the front door, but we do.

"I used to love Golden Apples," Aaron says, and his eyes get all dreamy.

I wait for an explanation, but all I get is a look of shock.

"You've never had Golden Apples?"

"I'm going to need you to stop saying 'Golden Apples,'" I say. "It sounds like something my grandma would make me eat."

I shake a crooked finger at him and try on my best old granny voice: "Eat your Golden Apples so you grow up big and strong, deary."

"These wouldn't make anyone big or strong. They were candy," Aaron says. "I don't know what they put in those things, but I wouldn't sleep for days after I ate one."

"Guess that explains why they stopped making them," I say, but Aaron doesn't respond. He just looks away.

The old Golden Apple factory doesn't look like much. I mean, it's an abandoned factory in the middle of the woods that miraculously only we seem to know about, so that's pretty cool. But besides the still-operational conveyor belt and overall creepy atmosphere that comes from any abandoned place, I can't figure out why Aaron was so stoked to show me the factory. It's virtually empty, and I'm starving. Plus, my parents would have been so happy that I've made a friend, they probably would have fallen all over themselves to feed us. Dad would have busted out the Suzy Q's for sure.

Maybe Aaron just wanted to get away from his house; I know I did—away from his dad, anyway.

"C'mon," Aaron says, waving me up a ramp and toward a back door with an unlit EXIT sign over it.

It's not an exit, though. Instead, the door leads to a hallway filled with more doors to the left and the right, each with at least two locks bolting them shut. A lockpick's dream.

"Whoa," I breathe, and Aaron nods.

"Each one leads to another door, too," he says. "All locked."

I stare at the corridor like we've uncovered a secret stash of Golden Apples.

"I've only made it through half of them. They've all got different brands of latches and padlocks. Here, I'll show you my favorite room."

Aaron beckons me to the middle of the corridor and fishes his tools from his pocket. Like me, he always carries his case. I hardly know what my pocket feels like anymore without it.

With his signature smoothness, he springs the first lock easily—a simple lever handle lock with a clutch. The door opens to a musty-smelling office, its furniture still haunting the room, waiting for its occupant to return. It's windowless, and the light switch doesn't work.

"None of 'em work," Aaron says. "I think the conveyor belt runs on an old generator or something."

In answer to our need, Aaron scoops up a heavy old flashlight from the top of a nearby filing cabinet.

"Found this baby on the first day," he says, illuminating his face from under his chin like he's about to tell me a ghost story. Then he twitches his eyebrows up and down. "Follow me."

I hear scurrying against the walls, and I know it's rats. I mean, it *was* a candy factory. I just pray to the Giant Aliens they keep to the walls and vents.

"What?" Aaron asks, his voice taunting. "You have a thing about rats?"

"I have a thing about rabies," I say.

"Hold this," Aaron says, handing me the flashlight. Then he fishes out a hook pick and leans his ear against the door. This is when I know Aaron is really at work; it's like he's listening to the door's heartbeat. I don't even bother asking why he locks the doors after he's sprung them open. It's because each time is like the first time, and there's no feeling like that.

With the tiniest flick of his wrist, the pin clinks, and the door groans open.

Inside is a treasure trove of broken machinery.

"I had a feeling you'd want to see this," he says, and I hardly know what to say.

There's this cartoon that I used to watch (okay, that I maybe, *possibly* still watch) with a ridiculously rich duck. He has so much money that he keeps all his gold and jewels and coins and bills piled in a room-sized vault, and he swims through the treasure like it's water. That's what I wanted to do when Aaron opened this door.

The secret office behind the regular office was probably considered a junk room, a kind of elephants' graveyard where electronics journeyed to eventually die as new hardware was invented to replace them. Maybe the tech guy at the Golden Apple Corporation figured he could make a buck selling those old monitors or keyboards or security cameras for parts. But the factory shut down, and the already-useless machines slept behind a locked door, guarded by an empty chair and another locked door.

"Dude, say something so I know you're not having a stroke or something."

"You smell like rat poop," I say, because it's the only way I can tell him no one has ever trusted me with treasure.

"Yeah. You're gonna want to scrape your shoes before you get home," he says, and I think he understands that "thank you" would be embarrassing.

I take what I can carry: the motor from an old vacuum, the fan from a CPU, a keyboard, and about five extension cords.

"I'll bring a bag next time," I say to Aaron, but he's already walking ahead of me, out the hallway and back onto the factory floor. He locks the door behind him so no one else can get in easily and vandalize our secret place. Before I know it, we're tromping over the wooded path that leads into the trees and away from the train tracks. Then he pauses, and I turn to see what it is he's staring at.

There, just over the tree line, is a red-and-gold seat, rocking and creaking on a mild breeze, attached to the top of a large metal arc.

"Is that a Ferris wheel?" I ask, already pushing past Aaron to cut a path through the overgrowth.

I'm expecting to find a clearing full of other confection-colored rides and ticket booths—one of the millions of county fairs that pop up on Main Streets or in open parking lots during the summer months—but what I find instead is a ghost town.

The Ferris wheel cars are paralyzed, moved only by the warm breeze that blows by. The wheel itself is covered in so much graffiti, I can't even tell what color it used to be. And not the cool kind of graffiti that's left by daredevil street artists. The ugly kind of graffiti that's meant to erase whatever's underneath. I see the opening to a fun house that looks more horror than fun with its apple-shaped head and its wide mouth with bared teeth. I see a charred concession stand that's missing its roof and a collapsed stage still encircled by tiered cement seats. There's a carousel of vandalized animals prancing across a motionless grate. There's the top curve of a roller coaster track cresting above the tree line, a lone car perched at the apex.

There used to be more—lots more. A directory obscured in oily burn residue tells me at least that much. But whatever this place was, it's dead and buried now.

Across the concession stand—in faded white letters over red paint—reads GOLDEN APPLE AMUSEMENT PARK.

"They made a park, too?" I ask, incredulous that Aaron didn't show me this just as eagerly as the factory. Sure, there were no locks or machines, but there is plenty to mess with between the Ferris wheel and the roller coaster. I mean, the cars have to be around somewhere.

"I bet I could get the carousel going again," I say, stacking my factory treasures against a tree and racing across the overgrown park.

I emerge from the brush to find him looking at the ground, his hands crossed over his chest. He's acting like he's mad at me.

"What's the matter?"

"Nothing, I just don't like it here," he says evasively.

"Are you joking? What's not to like? Seriously, why is this place, like, completely hidden?"

"It's not hidden," Aaron says, but he almost spits it out, like he's disgusted with me.

"Ooookay," I say, clearly terrible at sidestepping whatever land mine is buried under all this ash.

Ash. Like maybe it burned down.

"Did something . . . what happened here?" I ask, and Aaron looks up. His eyes look like they're ready to shoot lasers, and I'm close enough that I think he actually might throw a punch at me, but I still have no idea why.

Golden App
Honey Crisp Carousel
Hay Ride
Sidesh
Evil Orchard
Apple Picker
Apple Saucer

nusement Park
Rotten Core Rollercoaster
Wiggly Windy Worm Tunnel
Pink Lady Kids Hour
Cider Falls

Then he seems to catch himself and his shoulders relax a little. “I shouldn’t have come this way. I forgot this was here.”

But I don’t think that’s true. I think maybe he wanted me to see it.

“So did it, like, burn down or something?” I prod.

Aaron just stares at me.

“I lived down the street from a house that burned down once,” I say, starting to ramble. “It was a space heater or something, and everyone got out okay, but the house was completely torched, just like this . . . place . . . looks . . .”

I keep waiting for Aaron to say something—to save me from my babbling—but he keeps staring. The sudden silence is a stark contrast from the factory only moments ago. Just when I think we’re going to suffocate under all that awkwardness, Aaron shakes his head.

“Let’s get out of here,” he says, and even though I’m relieved to go, I know I’ve let Aaron down somehow. He doesn’t say a word the rest of the way home, just a casual “See ya around” before he steps onto his unlit porch and disappears into his house.

I replay the night in my head. The house with all its twists and turns. His dad’s . . . unique sense of humor. The factory. The amusement park. I try to figure out when things turned weird. Aaron was squirmy after we left his house, but that seemed to wear off once he showed me the factory. It was only after we got to the burnt remains of the amusement park that Aaron's entire demeanor changed. The guy who shared his trove of abandoned electronics had disappeared, and the angry, scared kid he'd left in his place needed me to know something.

"What were you trying to tell me, you weirdo?" I ask Aaron's dark porch, because I know what it's like to want someone to guess how you're feeling. It's way easier than saying it.

I set my electronics haul beside the door and decide I'll leave it there until the morning. Maybe by then I'll have a plausible explanation for where they came from. I barely have time to close the front door before Mom and Dad pounce on me.

"Did you have fun?"

"What's he like?"

"Are you in the same grade?"

"Have you had dinner yet?"

"Yeah, he's okay. Same grade," I say. Then I shrug. "Not hungry."

Mom's palm cups my forehead. "You coming down with something?"

"I just don't feel like eating, okay?"

Mom and Dad exchange a look.

"He *looks* like our son," Dad says, "but . . ."

He reaches for my face, tilting my chin to see up my nose, pinching my cheeks to open my mouth.

"I don't know, Lu. He could be a changeling."

"Hardy har har," I say, swatting Dad's hand away.

"Well, you have two choices," Mom says. "You can stay here and eat like a normal twelve-year-old or you can run a boring errand with your boring mother."

I hadn't noticed before that she's wearing her rain jacket and shoes.

"I need a book from my office," she says.

A book. From her office at the university.

"Your office is near the campus library, right?"

Mom cocks her head to the side. "Just the science library."

"But does it have newspapers? Like, old records?"

Mom looks like she wants to ask another question, then loses interest. "Probably," she says, grabbing her car keys.

* * *

Our shoes squeak against the orange-and-white linoleum of the Life Sciences building on the east end of campus. The university is old, and some of the original buildings are really pretty, all brick and dark wood and pillars. The east end of the grounds, though, was built sometime in the sixties, and I'm pretty sure that was the last time anyone's touched it. That's one of the reasons the school is so excited about having Mom on the faculty. She's a chemist, and not just any chemist. She's written a couple of papers on some experiment she did that got published in some hoity-toity journals, and now people know that Luanne Roth is super smart. Smart scientists mean more student enrollment, which means maybe the school will finally be able to buy some new equipment and remodel the bathrooms. Or so Dad says.

"Which way is the library?" I ask Mom.

"Downstairs, to the left, but, Narf, I'm only going to be a min—"

"Meet me down there!" I call over my shoulder, disappearing down the stairs and around the dark hallway before she can tell me no.

The science library is smaller than most elementary school libraries, which makes it easy to find the periodical section. Most of the tables are piled with neatly stacked science journals, well worn with sticky covers and dog-eared pages. Those aren't going to help me, though.

I keep scanning the periodical shelf until finally, in the very bottom corner, I spy a pile of old newspapers, the masthead on one I recognize from the sign on the building where Dad works: *The Raven Brooks Banner.*

I sit on the ground and pull the stack onto my lap, skimming through the headlines as quickly as I can for anything with the words "Golden" and "Apple." I'm a third of the way through the stack when I hear footsteps echoing through the hall above. I recognize my mom's urgent stride. Even when she's not in a hurry, she moves fast.

"Come on," I mutter, flipping faster through the pile, but nothing is jumping out at me. I skip to the bottom of the stack, but in my hurry, I fumble the papers and send the collection scattering.

"Narf, are you making a mess down there?"

I hear my mom's footsteps begin to descend the stairs. Ready to admit defeat, I start scooping the stack back together when I spy a paper with bold letters spelling out the headline.

I grab the paper and try to skim what I can, but Mom is almost at the bottom of the stairs. So I commit a mortal sin.

"Aliens, forgive me."

Tearing the newsprint, I pull the page from the paper and shove it into my pocket before my mom pokes her head around the corner.

"What were you trying to do, build a nest?" Mom asks, her hand massaging the back of her neck.

"I didn't tear anything!"

GOLDEN APPLE TRAGEDY
ONE YEAR LATER

I am, without a doubt, the world's worst criminal.

Mom knows it, too. She shakes her head at me, then helps me clean my mess before we leave the library mostly the way we found it.

At home, I wait until I can hear my parents snoring before pulling the article from my pocket.

On this day exactly one year ago, life for the Yi family changed forever, and the town of Raven Brooks lost a piece of its heart. What should have been a day of family fun at the newly opened Golden Apple Amusement Park turned to unimaginable tragedy when a mechanical flaw in the park's much-buzzed-about "Rotten Core" roller coaster caused the death of seven-year-old Lucy Yi.

A close-up picture of a smiling girl stares back at me from the page, her eyes sparkling under a fringe of dark bangs. I read the caption reluctantly:

Lucy Yi was a first grader at Raven Brooks Elementary School.

She *was* a first grader, I think to myself. Was, because she's dead now. Is that the something Aaron wanted me to guess? How could I ever have guessed something that horrific had happened right there in the same park where we were standing earlier tonight?

I keep reading.

"It was just so shocking. I mean, an amusement park is supposed to be a carefree place," says Trina Bell, a former

Golden Apple assembly line worker at the factory a mile from the park.

"I'll tell you this—no kid of mine is going to set foot on one of those contraptions ever again. This just goes to show you never really know what's safe," says Bill Markson as he sweeps the sidewalk in front of the Pup 'N' Puss Pet Supply. "You know what I think? I think they rushed to open before they'd done all those safety tests they should have done."

Yet not all of Raven Brooks blames the Golden Apple Corporation or the builders responsible for its construction. Gladys Ewing tries to hold on to the happy memories despite the long shadow cast by the confection maker's meteoric fall from popularity.

"I will never forget riding the Ferris wheel with my youngest son on opening day. I've never seen him smile that big. People ought to be ashamed of burning that place down like they did."

I read Gladys Ewing's quote three more times to make sure I've read it right.

"They burned it down?" I breathe.

In a week dominated by suffering for a family and reflection on the further tragedy that could have struck, angry parents and townspeople gathered at the shuttered Golden Apple Amusement Park to grieve together. But what was meant to be a candlelight vigil turned riotous when several disgruntled citizens turned their anger toward the park. By then, blame for young Lucy Yi's death had fallen to the Golden Apple Corporation and the amusement park's lead—

I flip the page over, but all I find are stories of the neighboring town's zoo and a sale on organic chickens at the natural grocer (when they were still selling meat, I suppose). I turn back to the article and see that the story continues on page B3.

I lay the crumpled newsprint at my feet and lean against the bed, my head all the way back as I stare up at the ceiling. So that's what Aaron couldn't find a way to tell me, not that I can blame him. How do you bring up something that awful in casual conversation?

As awful as the history of that place is, that isn't what's eating at me, either. What I can't figure out is why Aaron brought me there in the first place. He obviously wanted me to know what had happened there.

But why?

I fall asleep with thoughts of Aaron and his family whirling through my brain.

Mrs. Peterson's trembling hands as she puffed away on a cigarette by the window. The look she exchanged with Aaron when his dad talked about removing bones. The way

Mya's face lost all its color just before her dad picked her up and tickled her ribs.

That night, I dream of small, fragile skeletons crouched low to the ashy ground, bounding around a darkened Ferris wheel that's being slowly choked to death by vines.

CHAPTER 5

I don't exactly need another reminder that Raven Brooks is weird. Between the llama farm and the *not-quite-a-grocery-store*—not to mention the whole Golden Apple tragedy hidden in the woods—this town is bonkers.

"It's *eclectic*," Dad says as we pass a woman "walking" her dog in a baby sling.

"There's not a mall within thirty miles!" I complain.

"The Square has at least five stores that sell clothes."

"It's gonna be all organic cotton and canvas stuff." There's a display in the natural grocer with straw fedoras and scratchy hemp sandals.

"You don't know what it's going to be like until you see it," Dad says about the Square, but even he doesn't sound convinced.

"I'm going to look like freaking Davy Crockett on the first day of school. Why don't you just tie a piece of twine around my waist for a belt? It's bad enough Mom swapped my pudding packs for homemade granola. I'm not bringing that in my lunch, Dad. Seriously, it's not happening."

"Whoa, whoa," Dad says, looking both wounded and tickled. He pulls into a parking space in the Square and turns to me before I can escape the car.

"Where's all this coming from, Narf?"

I think about bolting, but I see Dad's finger on the power lock.

"I mean, I've barely met anyone yet," I say. "What if—" This is always the hard part: finding a way to tell my dad that I understand why we have to start over again, that I know it's not his fault that his job is hard to keep. It's just that every time we move, it gets harder to be invisible.

"Remember when we moved to Redding?" I ask Dad.

He nods, listening intently.

"Remember how I wore that Redding Rocks shirt on the first day?"

"The one with the granite?" Dad smiles. A good pun is never wasted on him.

But at school, a kid asked me if I shop for my clothes at the airport. I never told Dad about that.

"It's nothing," is what I say to him now. "But I draw the line at puns. No clever shirts."

Dad cocks his head to the side, but I get out of the car before he can prolong this conversation.

The Square really is a square. There's a giant copper fountain in the middle of it: Three enormous dancing apples with long, spindly arms and legs are supposed to look like they're playing, but the way their faces are carved makes them look almost vicious. It's super unsettling, but no one else seems to be as bothered as I am. Little kids fling pennies into the water and balance along the low brick wall that surrounds the sculpture.

Along the perimeter of the square, shops line up side by side facing the fountain. Restaurants ranging from casual to fancy make up the corners of each side, and the shops seem to be separated by theme: a side for really little kids, then kids my age, then adults, then the sort of catchall knickknack stores my mom would say are full of "more stuff I'll have to dust on a shelf."

"Oooh, they have a Wellington Hammel!" Dad's eyes sparkle against the reflection of the fountain as he gazes upon the expensive desk ornaments and massage chairs and rushes inside to join every other dad in Raven Brooks.

After twenty minutes, he's nearly convinced himself that he needs a stress-reducing foam figurine called *The Gnome,* when a guy I don't know comes up behind him.

"We've already got you stressed out enough for *The Gnome*?" he asks.

Dad turns and laughs, clapping the guy on the shoulder. "Even if you did, it's not like you're paying me enough to afford anything in this place!"

Now they're both laughing, and I see an equally uncomfortable kid lingering behind the guy who apparently knows how much money my dad isn't making at the *Raven Brooks Banner.*

He and my dad seem to suddenly remember us.

"And hey! This must be Enzo," my dad says, extending his hand to the kid, who takes it politely.

"Nice to meet you," the kid says. Then Dad pulls me forward and presents me.

"This is Nicky."

"Dad!" I cringe.

"Sorry, *Nick*. This is Nick. Narf, this is Miguel Esposito, the college roommate I told you and Mom about—the one who told me about the job."

"We were lucky your dad was available," says Miguel, and I can tell he's a nice guy because he finds an easy way around my dad's unemployment.

"Hey, Narf, I think you and Enzo are the same age. Eighth grade, right?" he asks Enzo, who nods.

"Maybe you two will share some classes," Mr. Esposito says, and Enzo and I look at each other and shrug. Parents always say stuff like that, then look at kids like we'll have the answers.

"If you like *The Gnome*, you should check out *The Gremlin*," Mr. Esposito says to Dad. "Twice the price, but it's a pen, too!"

They run off to play with their old people novelties and leave Enzo and me with exactly two things in common.

"I don't get it," says Enzo. "This is the same kind of garbage they sell in airplane catalogs, but Dad says those are a waste of money."

I chuckle like I've ever been on an airplane before. Anywhere we've ever gone has been a few days' drive away, and Dad and Mom never met a motel they didn't think was "charming." They're road-trippers, through and through.

"We're supposed to be buying me clothes," I say, and Enzo's nice like his dad because he doesn't ever flick his eyes down to see how worn my shirt is.

"C'mon," he says, walking ahead of me. "My friend's brother works at Gear, across the Square. He's always scoring us stuff for really cheap."

Gear doesn't look like the kind of place I should be shopping, but after Enzo has an exchange with the guy behind the counter who lifts his chin at me, Enzo tells me to grab a few shirts and pairs of shorts.

"Are you sure?" I ask, my embarrassment fighting it out with my ego because these clothes look normal, and they smell new, and at least I won't be wearing a blinking neon sign saying I'M NEW! on the first day of school.

"Yeah," says Enzo like it's no big deal. "This is pretty much the only place to shop around here. I mean, unless you want to rock a straw hat."

"Right. From the grocery store."

"Dude, I tried on those shorts once. It felt like I was wearing pants made of mosquitos. I was scratching my butt for weeks. People thought I had diaper rash."

He laughs, and holy Aliens this guy must be untouchable if he can survive a diaper rash rumor. It's weird, too, because aside from the normal clothes and gleaming white shoes, Enzo's just as much of a weirdo as me. It's nothing obvious, just something a fellow weirdo knows—his smile is totally unrestrained, he walks a little too fast.

We leave the clothes at the counter for my dad to buy later and head across the Square to the Gamers Grotto. I try to ignore the dancing apples in the fountain, but they're impossible to avoid.

"Creepy, right?" Enzo says.

"I thought it was just me."

"I don't know why they don't just take it down after what happened," he says, shaking his head.

I didn't make the connection until now—the dancing apples are an homage to the factory that built the park that left a hole in Raven Brooks wide enough to fall through. It seems like no matter how much I try to skirt the issue that no one wants to talk about, it's impossible not to topple down that hole. The tragedy of Golden Apple Amusement Park has clouded the entire town.

Now that I'm closer, I can see a small plaque has been added to the sculpture, a memorial protected behind glass. It's Lucy Yi, posed against a standard school-picture backdrop, her straight black hair smoothed behind a thin headband. Her hand is propped under her chin, a gold bracelet with a gleaming apple charm dangling from the links in a painful show of irony. Below her picture reads:

The sound of girls laughing wafts over my head, and for just a second, I swear it's coming from behind the glass of Lucy Yi's memorial.

Then one of them says, "I dare you to go say hi," and I look across the Square and see a group of younger girls crowded around a table at the frozen yogurt shop. The shortest one emerges, slapping one of her friends away, then brushing the hair from her face to wave to me. I recognize Mya and wave back before turning again to the fountain.

"Did you know her?" I ask Enzo. "The little girl who . . . ?"

Enzo looks down and nods. "Everyone did." Then he looks up with a crooked smile that doesn't quite reach his eyes, then in the direction of Mya and her friends. "Welcome to Raven Brooks, where everyone knows everyone." Then he claps me on the shoulder like his dad did to my dad and pulls me closer. "Whether you want to know 'em or not."

He chuckles, but I don't think he was kidding.

"But enough about that," he says. "Now, we game."

He'll get zero argument from me on that front. I may not know all there is to know about Raven Brooks or Golden Apples or expensive clothes, but I speak fluent Gaming.

Dad and Miguel lean against the coffee stand outside reliving their college days while Enzo and I fight for territory in *Mortal Realm* until my eyes blur. I've nearly forgotten that I'm the shiny new kid when I see Aaron from the corner of my eye entering the Grotto. He stalks in quietly, but I feel like the whole place comes to a standstill as soon as he steps through the door.

I lift my chin at him and give him a little half wave, but I don't think he sees me because he just walks behind a display of remote control cars locked in a glass case.

"You know him?" Enzo asks me, and I can't tell if he's impressed or disappointed.

"Yeah, he lives across the street from me," I say, watching Enzo carefully before adding, "He's cool."

Enzo doesn't say anything. He just sets the remote down on the console and edges around me to look for his dad.

"You guys hang out?" Enzo asks, not looking at me.

"Yeah," I say, knowing that's not the right answer, and I can feel the slim chance of normality slipping away from me. The thing is, up until now, Aaron's been the only one who actually wanted to hang out with me, and I'm not about to sell him out just because Enzo is . . . well, whatever Enzo is. I still can't get a read on what's bothering him about Aaron.

"Just watch your back around him," Enzo says, and all the confidence he exhibited earlier seems to melt away. That's what's bothering him—he's *afraid* of Aaron.

"What, does he kill cats or something?" I heard once that's how you know someone's going to be a serial killer.

"I don't know," Enzo says, and I swear to the aliens, he's actually not sure.

"He has, like, three cats around his house at all times!" I say, and I can't believe I have to convince Enzo that my new friend isn't a serial killer. "He's really nice," I say, although "nice" isn't quite how I'd describe Aaron now that I think about it. Still, he's no Jack the Ripper.

But it's clear to me that there's no convincing Enzo. He's already picking up his shopping bag and abandoning the game he was going to buy.

I follow him out the door and toward our dads, who have actual tears in their eyes from laughing so hard.

"Oh man, why has it taken us this long to get back in touch?" my dad says to Mr. Esposito, absently ruffling my hair.

"I don't know, but I'm glad you're here," Mr. Esposito says, and Enzo and I scuff our shoes on the ground until the dads finally give each other a half handshake, half hug, and say they'll see each other Monday.

"Did you find some clothes?" Dad asks, and I nod, guiding him toward Gear and away from Gamers Grotto, where I can't see Aaron at all anymore.

"Enzo seems nice," Dad says, and he's right. Enzo does seem nice. But I'm not thinking about how nice Enzo is right now. I'm thinking about how afraid he seemed of Aaron, how surprised he was that I wasn't afraid.

I pretend to be in a good mood on the way home, but I do it for Dad. I haven't seen him like this for a long time. When I get to my room, though, I don't even want to pull the tags off my new clothes or work on my audio manipulator (basically my coolest invention yet—to the untrained eye, it's a simple microphone, but when the unsuspecting speaker talks into the microphone, *bam!* Fart noises. It's part of my bodily functions line of inventions).

I was hoping that the trip to the Square would help me take my mind off of my bizarre night with Aaron, but between the fountain shrine to Lucy Yi and the way Enzo reacted to seeing Aaron, it's like the universe is begging me to relive it.

I keep thinking back to the look on Enzo's face when he saw Aaron, how he drew away from me when I told him we were friends. Sure, Aaron's family is a little weird, and his dad almost made me have an accident on their kitchen floor, but it wasn't Mr. Peterson who walked into the Grotto today. It wasn't Mr. Peterson I had to convince Enzo wasn't a serial killer. It was Aaron.

And if Enzo was afraid, it's hard for me not to wonder if I should be afraid, too.

CHAPTER 6

Aaron and I are doing reconnaissance, which is a cooler way of saying we're doing research. That might make my scientist mother and journalist father proud if it were reconnaissance for science or journalism.

But Aaron and I are doing research for my fart machine.

"Okay, walk me through it one more time," Aaron says.

"It's an audio-initiated voice manipulator programmed to distort the vocal reception based on tonal input."

It's by far my most sophisticated machine to date, something I haven't had a lot of time to play with ever since Aaron and I started spending every waking minute picking locks at the factory. To be honest, it feels good to be sharing something with Aaron that I know how to do better than him.

Aaron presses the top of his head like it hurts. "So how does it work?"

"I just told you," I say, trying not to get frustrated.

"No, you just said a bunch of words and strung them together into a sentence. That doesn't mean you explained anything."

"How do you know so much about locks and you can't follow the mechanics of an audio manipulator?"

"How do you keep talking so much without making any sense?"

"Boys, if you don't mind, I would prefer you maintain a peaceful tone in my store. My patrons have come to expect a heightened state of consciousness when they visit."

Aaron tries to stuff a laugh, but it escapes in a snort. I elbow his rib and shove him behind a display of healing crystals.

"Sorry, Mrs. Tillman."

The natural grocer is the first place our reconnaissance has taken us. We're in need of supplies, and we have reason to believe we'll find the best ones here.

Mrs. Tillman smiles a tight smile and turns with the stiffness of someone who commands herself to relax.

"Heightened state of consciousness?" Aaron hisses.

"Dude, quiet down."

"The only heightened anything in here are her wackadoodle prices. She used to buy goat cheese from the llama guy and let Girl Scouts sell cookies under her awning."

"Goat cheese?" I ask.

"Yeah, I guess he's got goats, too. Anyway, that's not the point," Aaron says. "She used to be nice. Then she goes to this silent retreat, doesn't talk for two weeks, and when she comes back, she's selling all these expensive, bogus vitamins and five-dollar 'candy bars.'"

He puts air quotes around "candy bars," and I have to laugh because this is the first time I've ever seen Aaron get vocally worked up about anything, and apparently he's got it out for phony, New Age capitalism.

I pick up a bar from a large endcap display. The bar is way heavier than it should be, and indeed it's marked $4.95, the word SURVIVA emblazoned across the packaging.

"Are these the fart bars?"

Aaron snorts again. "Yeah. Seriously, you've never smelled anything like it. Picture a toxic waste dump filled with dirty diapers in a sulfur pit."

We each grab three bars before making our way to the counter. It's six weeks' worth of allowance, but it's money well spent. All in the name of research.

"Thirty-two ninety-five," Mrs. Tillman says, this time not even bothering with her tight smile.

"Thanks, Mrs. Tillman," Aaron says, matching her frown with an extra-wide smile.

"The drugstore by the Square sells candy bars that might be more within your . . . budget," she says before handing us a paper bag, and this time she does smile.

On the way back to Aaron's house, I turn to him.

"So we'll be testing out the audio synthesizer—"

"At the natural grocer. Absolutely," Aaron says.

"Good," I say.
"Good," he says.

* * *

That night, after two Surviva bars and Mom's famous cabbage rolls, I'm passing enough gas to rocket me to Mars. If only my audio synthesizer were complete, I'd be able to test it. But like a dummy, I left my power drill at Aaron's house, and besides, he's the only one with a recorder.

Just then, like it can hear my thoughts, the high whir of a drill floats across the street from the direction of Aaron's house.

"Oh man," I grumble, stumbling toward the window. "You're gonna burn out the battery."

I haven't unpacked my charger yet, and because I sort of ignored Mom's warning to label all my boxes, it's anybody's guess where or when it'll turn up.

I cup my hands against the window and peer across the street to Aaron's room, but his bedroom light is off. If he's messing with my drill, he's doing it somewhere else in the house.

Since I'm way too bloated to go to sleep anytime soon, I slide my window open and pop the screen from its frame. The turquoise house came equipped with an unexpected bonus right outside my room—a trellis sturdy enough to act as a ladder. I'm not exactly the kind of kid who sneaks out of the house when his parents are sleeping, but it's just across the street, just to retrieve my drill. Besides, it's easier than waking my parents up and explaining why I need the drill anyway.

I hear the whir of the drill again, but it stops by the time I'm across the street. The streetlight in front of my house flickers, and for a second, I'm standing on Aaron's lawn in the dark. It's the first time I've been here this late at night, and it occurs to me that I haven't been invited. The light in Aaron's room is still off, and suddenly, it feels like I've gone from hanging out to trespassing.

The drill revs up again, and I see the faintest light seeping out from the crack of the basement door. The streetlight flickers back on, and I find myself standing closer to the boarded-up basement door than I realized I was. I peer closer at the myriad of locks, only what I see now that I'm closer is more unsettling than any lock.

There are handprints all over the door, smears of black grease that creep around the edge of the door, half covered by the boards and bolts, some with tiny scratches at the tips of the fingerprints, like claw marks made by dragging fingernails.

Suddenly, the drill's motor cuts out, and the whir sputters, the telltale sign of a dying battery. Then a heavy footfall lands on the steps leading up from the basement, methodically making their way up the stairs.

Straight for the door.

I bolt as fast as I can across the street, the streetlight clicking off just as I reach my house, and all at once, I can't see the trellis against the wall. I hear the rattle of locks behind me, thumping against the heavy basement door as they're slowly unlocked.

Groping through the vines in my front yard, I finally find a wooden slat and grab hold of it, wedging my foot in the one beside it before pulling myself up into the window. I reach the ledge of my windowsill just as the streetlight clicks on again.

Just as I hear the basement door swing open behind me.

I don't turn around. I fall through the open window and take cover on the floor, my heart pounding against the floorboards as I listen for movement across the street.

Heavy footfalls thud against the grass, muffled in the humid, still night. The air is so dense, it feels like whoever is across the street is stealing my breath.

The footsteps leave the grass and move to the sidewalk, closer, their soles cracking over the tiny pebbles on the asphalt. I squeeze my eyes shut and wait for whoever is outside my window to say something, to clamp on to the trellis and climb into my room, to laugh. To do anything at all.

Instead, the person with the heavy step stands perfectly still in the middle of the road, waiting.

I don't know how much time passes. Maybe a minute,

maybe an hour. All I know is that just when I think I'm going to die of suffocation from all that thick air, the steps recede to the sidewalk, then to the lawn, then to the basement door, where the hinges creak to a close and the locks secure whatever secret is worth locking up in Aaron's basement.

I peer over the windowsill, and when I'm sure no one is still lying in wait in the middle of the street, I resecure my screen and close my window. I lock the latch, but I wish I had a few more locks than that.

It wasn't Aaron, I'm positive of that. Whoever wanted me to know they knew I was there, they had a much heavier step, a heavier frame.

"Bigger bones," I whisper, and a chill rattles my whole body.

Because whatever Mr. Peterson is doing in his basement, he wants to be sure I know it's none of my business. There's no doubt in my mind—tonight was a warning from my new friend's dad.

And Mr. Peterson doesn't strike me as the type to warn someone twice.

CHAPTER 7

The rattle on my trellis wakes me from a restless sleep.

It was the grocery store again, the cold metal grid of the cart against my bare legs. The towers of canned goods. The giant brown doors with their rubber stoppers on the ground. I got out of the cart this time, and when I pushed the doors open, I didn't see the grocery aisles that I thought I would. It was just endless tunnels in every direction—dark, winding passages leading to nowhere. I've never felt more afraid.

I overheard my grandma once say to my mom, *Keep a leash on that wolf. He sees too much at night*. For as much as I've always hated my nightmares, my grandma hated them more, which is strange because I never even told her about them. She always just knew. I wish my mom had figured out how to put that leash on me.

Between the nightmare and the specter of Mr. Peterson still too close to ignore, I launch myself from my bed and head straight for the window, determined to face down whatever threat is rattling the trellis.

Except there's no one there.

"Must have been a cat," I tell myself. The neighborhood cats have taken to climbing the trellis lately, a fun new development to set my already frayed nerves on edge.

I'm just about to go back to bed when I hear the crinkle of paper. I open the window and lift the screen from the frame, leaning as far as I can over my window without falling out. There, trapped between a rung of the trellis and the vines that weave through it is a carefully folded piece of notebook paper.

I teeter out onto the trellis, still shaky from my dream, and my foot loses its grip on the slat just above the piece of paper. I catch myself, but barely, and I'm rewarded with a sharp scratch from a splintered adjacent rung.

I grasp the note, holding it in my mouth until I've climbed back to my window and replaced the screen.

8:00 PM. Llama Farm.
Don't be late.

I smile, even though my hands are still shaking from my climb and my arm is burning with a new scrape and my head is still swimming with visions of dark, endless tunnels.

* * *

I arrive at 7:59. Aaron is already there, lying in wait, pick in hand.

"Ready?" he asks.

"I have no idea," I say.

"Well, just answer me this: Can you be stealth?"

"Um . . . yes?"

"I need a firm commitment here, Nicky."

I've never seen Aaron more serious, which is why I can't keep myself from laughing.

"Dude, this is mission-critical, Navy SEAL–level action. I need to know—are you in?"

I pull myself together as best I can. "Let's do this."

Here's the thing—once Aaron discovered I was good with gadgets, a world of opportunity in this strange yet boring town seemed to open up. Cranky Mrs. Bevel restores old doll heads, so of course we had to find a way to pipe creepy voices into her shop. Look, if you're going to own a store filled with antique doll parts, you're kind of already set up for terror. It was so easy once Aaron convinced her he was looking for something to replace the head on his mom's broken Madame Alexander doll; I put a plug here and a switch there, and poof—haunted doll heads chanting: "We're lonely" and "Come play with us."

And Mr. Quinn lets his dog poop on Aaron's lawn practically every morning, and he never picks it up. All Aaron had to do was throw a ball into his backyard to get Mr. Quinn to step away from his mailbox for a few minutes. It was the perfect opportunity to test out my spring-loaded catapult in his mailbox. The weapon of choice—a nice, soft ball of dog turd—was really just poetic justice.

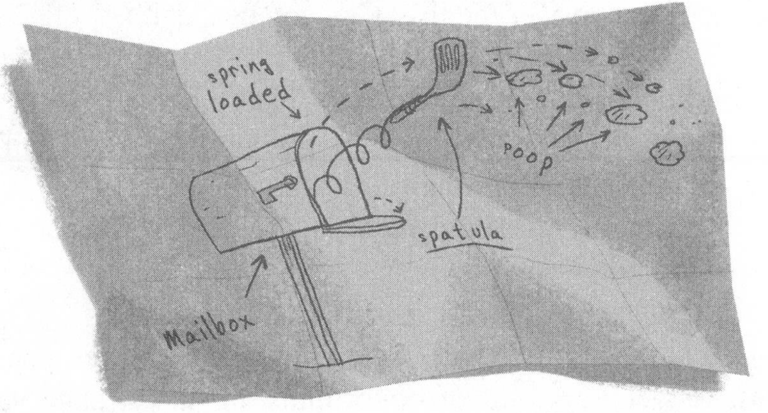

Anyway, as far as I can tell, Farmer Llama never did anything deserving of the Robin Hood–level justice we've been doling out, so I'm not altogether certain what we're doing here. But Aaron is 100 percent dialed in, and he's not in a place to be questioned at this second.

Aaron spends half his time looking over his shoulder, even though I'm the lookout.

"Just focus on the lock," I say.

"Gimme some space. Any closer, you'll be on my shoulders," he says, and holy Aliens, Aaron is nervous. This is the first time I've ever seen him nervous during a prank.

"You know we're both going to be in so much trouble if we get caught, right?" I say, wiping a bead of sweat from my hairline.

"Nope," he says. "Not getting caught."

"C'mon, you can't pull a prank on a llama farm without attracting attention. Llamas are too cute. Mess with llamas, pay the consequences. It's just common sense," I ramble.

"Number one," he says, "no one ever said anything about doing anything to the llamas. We're after something of more . . . symbolic value. The llamas are off-limits."

"Try the bump key," I say, and Aaron looks annoyed, but he tries it anyway.

"Number two," he continues, "I thought you only answered to your space alien overlords."

"True," I concede. "We are ruled by a race of distant Space Overlords who will one day rain down their fury upon us lowly earthlings. So I guess we might as well seize the day?"

"I still don't get it," he says. "I thought your family was Jewish."

"We are."

"So you guys, like, believe that we're ruled by aliens?"

"I'm sure I could convince at least one rabbi that it's a possibility."

I crowd him again. "Maybe you should use the rake. The bump isn't going to work." Aaron positions a hammer over the key. "You're never going to get the leverage you need with that," I say.

"I don't need leverage," he says, "when I've got torque." He takes a deep breath and brings the hammer down on the key. With a thud, the old padlock drops to the ground.

Aaron smiles. "By my count, that's three for me and one for you this week."

"Hey, as far as I can tell, you've got zero excuse for not being a master lock-breaker by now. You've got a house full of locks! Jeez, you could practice on that basement door outside your house and become a pro in a day if you weren't so lazy."

Somewhere along the way we must have stopped joking, though, because by the time I turn around, Aaron's face has turned to stone.

"What?" I ask, a knot forming in my stomach.

"Nothing. Let's just get this over with, okay?" he says, and I open the gate with far less joy than I felt a minute ago.

The tension is short-lived, though. The enormity of our mission unfolds before us once we're in Farmer Llama's field.

Aaron looks at me. "Stealth," he whispers.

I nod in response.

We make our way along the fence line, wary of the farm owner whose name we don't know, so we've just been calling him Farmer Llama. He's rarely seen in public, occasionally at the natural grocer (evidently, he's not the type to hold a grudge) or out in the field grumbling at them, and I swear to the Aliens they sound like they grumble back. What's got me on edge is that, unlike Mr. Quinn or Mrs. Bevel, we haven't been able to assess Farmer Llama's comings and goings.

"What if Farmer Llama's in the barn?" I whisper.

"Then we took a wrong turn." Aaron shrugs.

"Through his padlocked chain-link fence?"

We take a few more steps before Aaron hisses, "Heads up!"

We fall to the ground like snipers behind a barricade. Footsteps approach quickly, their pace increasing the closer they get. I ready my excuses.

We're selling candy for our baseball league.

We're with the Future Farmers of America.

We want to mow his lawn.

"This is it," I whimper. "Mom, Dad, I love you. Please don't send me to military school."

"Quiet," Aaron whispers, but he's laughing so hard he farts, and now I can't keep it in, and oh well. It was a good life, I suppose.

The footsteps come to an abrupt halt a couple of yards away.

Aaron rises from the grass first and snorts.

I stand to find myself eye-to-eye with a dusty gray llama.

"Why do they sound so human when they walk?" Aaron asks.

"I've asked myself that same question so many times."

"C'mon," Aaron says, dusting off the grass. "Let's just—"

"Ignore the llama?"

"Right," he says.

I salute him. "Roger that." I nod. "Stealth."

The llama burps.

"So what are we looking for?" I ask.

"The barn," Aaron says, and we both look at the field in front of us. I count five barns, all identical in size and faded shade of blue.

"Can you be more specific?"

"I . . . uh . . ."

More footsteps, and out of the tall grass emerges a dark brown llama to accompany the first.

"Hey, look, he brought a friend!" I say.

"Can we focus, please?" Aaron says, and I can tell he's getting nervous again, but I can't help myself. We make it halfway across the field before we realize we've attracted a small crowd. At least five llamas follow us toward a small blue outbuilding at the edge of the field.

I can't contain my laughter.

"What?"

"I think we left *stealth* back there by the gate. In case you hadn't noticed, we've got groupies now."

A llama sneezes, spraying the side of my arm.

"Anyway, we're almost to the barn, right?" I say.

But just as we approach the outbuilding, I hear a voice in the distance.

"Maggie! Frank? What the dickens are y'all doing out there?"

At first I think he's talking to us, but two of the llamas turn in his direction when they hear his voice.

"Shoot! Go go go!" I drop to the ground and army crawl on the itchy grass toward the little blue building.

"Joey! Cindy! Where the devil are you?"

I keep expecting people to pop out of the nearby buildings, but no, clearly Maggie, Frank, Joey, and Cindy are the llamas steadily chewing a path at our tail, giving away our location with every second they linger.

"Now or never, Nicky," Aaron whispers, and this time I can tell he's not goading me on. Whatever this stupid mess is, we're in it together.

I crawl until my pants fill with dry grass, and in an act of awesome bravery (okay, pointless idiocy), I leap to a stand and swing around the corner of the outbuilding, Aaron following close behind.

We stand there panting, backs against the clapboard wall of the barn, and all at once, I see Aaron's eyes light up in the dark.

"What?" I ask under my breath.

"That's it," he says, and his face breaks into a smile.

I can't see what he's so happy about. It's just the inside of a barn wall. But whatever it is, it's what we came here for tonight.

Seconds later, I hear heavy boots crush the overgrowth where we were just hiding.

"It's dinnertime," a gravelly voice says from so close by, I can hear him wheeze.

We go silent, not even daring to exhale. I squeeze my eyes shut, willing myself to be invisible.

One of the llamas grunts.

"Now don't you take that tone with me," Farmer Llama says, and I elbow Aaron hard in the ribs while he bites his hand to keep from losing it.

More shuffling in the grass, and finally, one of the llamas offers a more agreeable sound.

"All right, that's more like it," he says, and his boots kick their way through the tall grass. One by one, his llamas follow their master, grumbling as they go.

Once we're sure he's left the barn, and we can't hear the llamas nearby, Aaron emerges from the barn first, signaling me to head through the stall to the area he was smiling at a minute ago.

We stare down at it, a pile of identical tin signs stacked high in the corner of the barn.

"What did he even need this many for?" Aaron asks.

I look anxiously over my shoulder at the barn door. "You're sure he's not going to miss it?"

"Nicky, he has like a million," he says, and I know he's right, even if what we're doing feels a little wrong.

We keep off the main roads, snaking through side roads and side yards, avoiding streetlights like kryptonite, the sign tucked under my arm as I bring up the rear while Aaron forges a safe path.

Back at home that night, I scratch my belly raw. Little red bumps have begun to spring up, and I finally have to ask Mom where the cortisone cream is.

"What in God's name did you do to yourself?" She gasps, reaching for the scratches as I yank my shirt down.

"Poison oak," I say, which is completely unsatisfactory.

"Poison oak? But it's only on your stomach." She side-eyes me.

"It's personal, okay?" I invoke the ultimate excuse, the explanation that kills any adolescent inquiry dead.

Mom backs away with her hands up. "I don't want to know."

It's my second victory of the day.

I wait until I hear the television click off in my parents' room and their soft, intermingled snoring fills the air before I pull the dented tin sign from under my bed.

I gaze upon my prize:

We had no choice but to take the sign; it was literally calling my name.

But actually, it called to Aaron first. It was my name, and he answered the call, planning a heist that would only have special meaning for me.

We've never stayed in one place long enough for me to make a good friend. That night, I toss and turn, worried about how long it will take for my family to leave Raven Brooks, just like we've left everywhere else.

CHAPTER 8

By late July, we've picked our way through most of the locks at the Golden Apple factory. I've gotten almost as good as Aaron, but I don't feel the need to tell him that. He already knows. Most of the time, I think he's glad about it, but sometimes—like today—I think maybe he's jealous.

Imagine that. A kid jealous of Nicholas Roth. The new kid. The Narfinator. The one who knows every *Twilight Zone* episode by heart (thanks, Dad) and every element on the periodic table (thanks, Mom). The one who likes sushi better than cheeseburgers and likes girls who are taller than him and thinks Talking Heads is still the best band there ever was, I don't care what anyone says.

"You planning to bust that lock this century, or should I start rationing food?" Aaron says behind me.

Yeah. He's jealous.

"I told you to eat your breakfast," I say in my best mom voice.

"Eat this," he says, leaning in to punch me in the shoulder, but I spring the lock just in time to swing open the door, and he stumbles through and lands squarely in a pile of bubble wrap packing. It seems we've found the shipping department.

I laugh so hard I think I'm going to rupture something, and eventually Aaron laughs, too.

"Welp, nothing to see here," I say, shoving a box of packing peanuts aside.

"Not so fast," Aaron says, mesmerized as every human on earth is by the simple act of popping a sheet of plastic bubbles.

Once we exhaust an entire roll of bubble wrap, we both are really hungry, and we make our way back to the room that used to be the elephants' graveyard of electronics before we picked it clean. Now we refer to it as the Office. We left an operating TV and VCR in there after we discovered that the generator that powers the conveyor belt powers electricity for some of the second-floor offices as well. Aaron's amassed a sizeable library of movies thanks to an obsession he has about recording them when they air. His timing for catching the best movies is freakishly good. Throw in a couple of cushy executive chairs pilfered from the nicest offices and we have our very own media room.

Aaron rummages around in a filing cabinet and pulls out a bag of cheese crackers and a couple of sodas.

“You seriously have rations?” I say, tearing into the crackers. I pause for a second when I hear skittering behind the wall beside me. Great. Now the rats know we have crackers.

“I like to be prepared,” Aaron says. “The end is nigh.” He laughs a ghoulish laugh and I roll my eyes, and things feel normal again. As normal as they can around Aaron.

That’s why it feels like the right time to ask him about how everyone acted when he walked into the Gamers Grotto at the Square. It’s been a few weeks, but I haven’t been able to shake the memory.

“I went clothes shopping with my dad,” I offer.

“Sounds riveting,” he says.

“It was all right. A kid named Enzo hooked me up with some pretty cool stuff,” I say, easing into what I really want to ask him.

Aaron doesn’t say anything, though. He just fiddles with the metal tab on his soda can.

"I think he said he knows you," I say, trying again.

This time Aaron looks up. "He doesn't know anything."

Just like that, I've hit a nerve. Instead of backing off, I decide to press on it.

"Yeah, so what's up with the way everyone seems . . . I don't know . . ."

He eyes me carefully.

"Weird around you," I say, but that's not really what I want to say. I want to say "*scared* around you." I want to ask him why *I'm* not afraid of him. I want to ask him if that makes me a chump, the would-be victim of a C-list horror movie.

"You didn't, like, kill a cat or something, did you?" I ask, and I don't know how to follow that up, so I say, "'Cause I like cats."

Aaron looks at me like the Aliens have already arrived, like I'm their alien spawn, like I have tubes for ears and antennae for eyes and a long, forked tongue that I use for catching and eating the human race I used to be a part of.

"Why would I kill a cat?" he asks, and *his* question lays bare how stupid *my* question sounds.

"I don't know," I say lamely.

"Enzo stopped hanging out with me because he'd rather play video games," Aaron says quietly, wiggling the tab of his soda can until it comes off. He flicks it across the room into an old waste basket.

He doesn't have to say any more. I can hear every single word he's left out—Enzo would rather play his expensive video games that his successful dad can buy him because his dad has a job, and that job isn't going away. It's yet one more thing I can't figure out how to bring up with Aaron—that his dad is always around, even during the day, like how my dad is around all day when he's between jobs.

There are reasons why the Enzos of the world don't hang out with the Aarons and the Nickys of the world. They don't have to be good reasons or fair reasons. But there are always reasons.

Too bad, I think. Enzo seemed okay.

I let out a massive belch that echoes across the empty factory floor. "I don't even like video games that much," I say.

It's a humongous lie, and Aaron knows it, but for the first time all day, he looks relaxed, like a tiny bit of the twelve-year-old he is has started to seep back in.

Later at Aaron's house, though, the lightness that seemed to free Aaron of some massive burden that afternoon disappears once again under the weight of his family. Everyone at the Peterson house is in a bad mood.

I thought it was just his mom, who met us at the door, then floated away without saying a word. Then, after taking too much time removing my rat poop shoes and placing them outside the door, I lost track of Aaron and practically ran straight into Mya in the hallway. She was looking over her shoulder, and when she turned and saw me, she jumped back about a foot.

"Jeez, Nicky, don't be such a creeper!"

"I'm not—"

"I have to go," she said, hurrying out the door with one more furtive glance over her shoulder, not at me but behind me. I turned to see what she was looking for, but all I saw were the shadows that lie in the twists and turns of the Petersons' house.

Now, as we sit in Aaron's room tinkering with the lock on an old chain we scrounged from a construction site, I wait for Aaron to say something. *Anything*. Because we've been sitting here in dead silence for over an hour.

"My parents got a letter from the school. I have my class schedule, but I don't know who any of the teachers are, so it's pretty much meaningless."

"Mmm," Aaron grunts.

"I had a Life Sciences teacher at my last school," I say. "She had this thing about rabbits. Like, she had about a dozen at home, and she was constantly worrying about them. Sometimes she even brought them to class because she was afraid they'd be lonely, but I always kinda thought it was more so *she* wouldn't be lonely . . ."

"Uh-huh."

"So yeah, I thought that was weird . . ." I clear my throat.

Aaron stares out the window.

"The Alien Overlords came to see me last night. They brought me aboard their vessel and threatened to melt my brain into soup unless I promised to become a secret alien agent and share top secret human intelligence with them."

"Yup," Aaron mutters, still staring out the window.

"So then you'll help me?"

"Huh?"

"Become an alien-human double agent."

"Man, what are you talking about?"

"What's up with you? You've been out of it ever since we left the factory," I say.

Aaron looks back out the window. I'm about to give up and go home when he says, "Have you ever thought that maybe you were . . . ?"

"What?"

"Nothing, never mind," Aaron says, looking down.

"What? Like . . . a merman? No, no, I've never thought that maybe I was a merman. I mean, I like to swim and all. I'm not half bad at it, either. There was this lake near—"

Aaron chuckles despite himself. "Weirdo."

"Now *that*, yeah. I've thought I was a weirdo before. Often, actually."

Aaron finally looks at me.

"Have you ever thought you were . . . bad?"

It sounds like such a simple question. I know it should

have a simple answer. But Aaron and I both know it's not that simple.

"I mean, we play pranks on people. I think that's probably not *upstanding-citizen good*," I say, Mom's refrain of using my powers for good once again pushing its way into my mind.

"No, but I mean *really* bad," Aaron says, looking back down at the floor.

My dream washes over me, the one I have practically every night but try not to let myself remember during the daytime, the one in the store surrounded by food lined up on the shelves. The room is dark. I'm alone.

And even though I have no idea why, I know beyond a doubt that it's my fault I'm there.

"I think I did something bad once."

I say it before I know I'm saying it. It's like I'm hearing myself talk from across the room.

"You don't know?" Aaron asks, looking hard at me now, searching me for a lie.

"I don't remember," I say, a truth I've never admitted to anyone before. "It's just this dream I have. It changes sometimes, but I always wind up in the same place, like I was put there or something."

"So how do you know you did something wrong?" Aaron asks.

I think about it for a minute, and when my brain quiets to

a whisper, all I hear is my grandmother's voice. *You stop that wandering, or one day, you won't make it home.*

"Because sometimes I go where I'm not supposed to," I say. "Sometimes, I go too far."

Now we're both looking out the window, and I wonder what Aaron's bad dreams look like, if he feels as alone in his as I do in mine.

"I don't think just because you do bad things, it makes you a bad person," Aaron says after a long stretch of silence.

All of a sudden, it occurs to me that I still haven't found out why Aaron was so weird about the Golden Apple Amusement Park last month. My mind is racing with thoughts of a prank gone awry. Could Aaron have done something to the roller coaster that made it crash? But I stop myself before I get too far—pulling a prank is one thing, but bringing down a roller coaster at nine years old? It's not possible. But if he's not talking about that, then what is he talking about?

"What *does* make a person bad, then?" I ask.

Aaron shoves his hands in his pockets like he's embarrassed. Then, so quietly I can barely hear him, he says, "Being happy when bad things happen."

I watch Aaron's face for any clues into what he could mean, but his expression is as flat as his tone.

Then he looks at me and smiles, and it's the old Aaron again, the one who planned a mission just for me to get a sign with my name on it, who carved a safe path through the town of Raven Brooks just so I could get home safely with a two-by-two-foot tin treasure.

He's my friend. An *actual* friend. Whatever he did or thinks he did, I've got his back.

"I'm hungry," I say. "Let's go get some tacos."

CHAPTER 9

That night, I lie in bed waiting for sleep to come, but my stomach is churning. I don't know if it's the tacos or the fact that my conversation with Aaron brought my brain back to the Golden Apple Amusement Park. I just can't seem to stop imagining what it was like when that roller coaster car went rocketing off the tracks into a tree. I must be the only twelve-year-old in the world who keeps a newspaper clipping of a tragic accident by his bed. It's become a habit to reread the same half article at night, skimming it for clues I may have missed before. I haven't had a good excuse to get back to the library at the university since I hitched a ride with Mom last time, so the second half of the story is still a mystery.

Maybe I'm waiting for it all to make sense; maybe I don't actually want to know how the story ends. I think about how scared that little girl must have felt, what the other people on the roller coaster thought when it detached, if they even knew or just kept rolling along wondering what everyone was screaming about. I think about what my parents would have done if it was me. The only time I've ever seen my mom cry was when Grandma died. I wonder if she'd cry that hard if I died like Lucy Yi.

I've just accepted the reality that I'm probably going to throw up, when a scream cracks the night and launches me from my bed.

I rush to the window and press my forehead against the glass, looking for what could have made such an anguished sound. It came from across the street, I'm positive of that. And though it sounds totally nuts, I'd swear it sounded like Aaron's voice. I've never heard him scream, and anyway what would make him do that at two in the morning?

But there was something in the tail end of that wail that sounded so familiar.

I stare out the window for so long that my breath starts to fog the glass. Nothing follows that one unearthly sound but a swath of silence not even pierced by a yowling cat or skittering leaf.

Maybe I did fall asleep, I tell myself. I'd been so wrapped up in thoughts of morbid accidents and crying moms that I dreamt the scream.

I'm not satisfied with that answer, but my stomach is starting to churn again, and I'm getting sweaty with my breath bouncing off the window onto my face.

I open the window to get a little fresh air, and the silence of the night is once again interrupted, this time by the faint but undeniable sound of music.

Ice-cream-truck music.

Across the street, light glows from the crack under the Petersons' boarded-up basement door. I start to have flashbacks of that night I eavesdropped on the side of Aaron's house—the night Mr. Peterson lurked outside my window in wordless warning—but a memory more powerful than that is driving me now. The memory of that scream that woke me up, but somehow didn't stir the rest of the neighborhood, just like the music doesn't.

I fight back the voice of logic begging me to stay in my room and not pop the screen from the window frame. The trellis is beginning to get rickety from all this climbing, but I don't care about that now. All I care about is getting close to the Petersons' house. Maybe I can just get a sign from Aaron that everything is okay, that whatever is going on in his basement is totally innocent. The drilling, the music, the screams—they're all just . . .

Just what? A play rehearsal? A murder mystery party? All just some comical misunderstanding invented by the short kid across the street with the grubby shoes?

The dew from Aaron's lawn soaks my feet, and I stand underneath his window, the crooked oak tree releasing tiny droplets onto my head. I scour the yard for a small pebble to chuck at Aaron's window, and after a few failed attempts, I land one right on the glass. I flinch at the sound, then wait for him to wake up and tell me to leave him alone. Nothing would be more comforting right now. Instead, Aaron's room remains dark, and the music from the basement cuts in and out like skips on a record player, setting my nerves further on edge.

"C'mon," I plead with Aaron under my breath, giving his window one more try, but this time, I throw the pebble a little too hard, and instead of a pinging sound, I hear a pop, then a crack, and I realize with horror that I've splintered Aaron's window.

The music in the basement cuts off, and the footsteps don't just fall evenly on the stairs like they did last time; now they pound up the steps, thundering the shortest warning before the jingling of keys signals the furious unlocking of the dead bolts securing the door.

Frantic, I realize that this time, I won't have a chance to get across the street undetected. The house offers no place to hide, no bush for cover or garage for shelter. The only place to go is the backyard.

I regain movement and bolt for the backyard with the kind of adrenaline you hear about in moments of crisis. Evidently, I have more power in my skinny legs than I realized. I lunge for the only cover I can see—a pair of oak trees directly behind the house that make for the worst hiding place ever, but I don't have a choice because the keys are rattling faster now and the door is starting to move from its frame.

Just as I pull myself behind the trunk, a loud bang on the basement door makes my heart catch in my throat. I peer through the leaves and realize that one lock is still in place, and rather than patiently unlock it, whoever is behind the door has given up trying and is instead throwing himself against the wooden door.

Flinching with each violent knock, I watch as the door bends behind the weight of the attack, the tiny crackling of splintering wood sending a chill through my paralyzed body. With one more vicious thrust, the last stubborn lock falls to the grass, and a hulking Mr. Peterson falls through the doorway, red-faced and sweating, with a foam of white spittle gathering in the corners of his mouth.

I hang on to the trunk of the oak tree and plead silently with my heart to stop pounding for fear that the animal that has taken over Mr. Peterson will hear it with his supersonic hearing. I'm quaking so hard, I can see the leaves above me trembling, and I pray not a single leaf drops.

I watch in terror as Mr. Peterson skulks across the yard in search of the sound that interrupted his work. I can hear him panting from here, and I begin to think the craziest thoughts:

How my last meal will have been tacos.

How disappointed Mom will be in me for using my powers for eavesdropping.

How I'll never have gotten to test out my audio manipulator.

How through this entire horrific episode—through the drilling and the window breaking and the door destroying—Aaron and his family have managed to stay quietly tucked into their beds, unaware that the boy across the street is about to be annihilated by their psycho dad.

I watch as Mr. Peterson crouches to the grass and examines what I can only guess are the footprints I left in the dew. And that's when I notice that there's a grave. Well—I'm not sure it's really a grave because there isn't a dead body in it—but it definitely looks like a grave. Mr. Peterson stands slowly, tromping his way across the lawn, and now his demeanor has calmed a bit, as though the animal inside him has been suddenly tamed. He picks up the shovel and starts filling in the grave, even though I swear there's nothing in there. Just an empty, grave-shaped hole that I assume he buries trespassers like me in.

Ten minutes pass, then twenty, then thirty as my legs feel weaker and weaker. Suddenly I come back to my senses as the shoveling stops and Mr. Peterson steps to the sidewalk and then to the middle of the street, staring up at the window to my room, looking for signs of life there instead of behind him in his own tree.

I swallow to wet my dry throat, but it's no use. I've sweat every ounce of moisture from my body. I'd pee my pants if I wasn't already as dry as a desert.

Then, just like last time, Mr. Peterson satisfies whatever

compulsion he had in staring down my bedroom window, and once again, he cuts a path through his lawn, stopping one more time to stare at the dented grass by the side of his house.

I'm positive he's about to see me. Even with the trunk providing cover, there's no doubt he'll spot my stupid teal shirt through the camouflage. I brace for my fate, the adrenaline no longer providing me strength. Now all I can do is wait in paralyzed silence to be discovered.

But Mr. Peterson doesn't look up. Instead, he walks calmly, almost serenely, through the basement doorway, closing the door with care and methodically locking the bolts that remain in place after the carnage.

I wait until I'm sure it's not a trap. I wait for the music that doesn't start up again, for the sound of shoes that don't touch the basement steps, for the cracked window in Aaron's room to open. I wait for a single sign of life in the house that was moments ago alive with the fury of a single hulking monster.

Then I come out. I dread climbing the trellis and consider sleeping in my backyard just so I can hide. When I do make it to my room, I push my dresser in front of the window as a barricade.

When I wake up the next morning, I feel braver somehow. Maybe it's the light of day creeping in around the sides of my dresser or the soreness in my arms that reminds me I had enough wits about me to hide behind the tree. Whatever the reason, I lean against my dresser and return it to its place, staring at the house that had terrified me so badly under the cloak of midnight.

"You're not so scary," I tell the house and the man inside it, and I almost believe myself until I flinch a little too hard at the sound of scratching just below my window.

There, tucked into the trellis propped against the exterior under my bedroom window, is a folded piece of yellow notebook paper, its edges fluttering and scraping the siding in the morning breeze.

Retreating back to my room, I rummage through my box of gadgets until I find what I'm looking for, a handy little tool I invented after realizing the tangle of vines on the trellis was where Aaron would be leaving me all my secret messages. I finally find it, the grabber I customized using the extender from a pool broom and the lever from a pooper-scooper. Then I return to the window, carefully lowering the grabber and retrieving the paper from the vines.

But when I unfold the paper to read its message, I feel even worse than I did when I woke up on the floor.

I look out the window across the street and wait for the messenger to make themselves known, but I know it's no use. It appears they left behind more than a note, though. From the ground, a glinting catches my eye. I squint to see what it is, but the sun reflects off its surface, and I can't make it out.

"Guess I'm climbing you again after all," I say to the trellis, which groans under my weight.

At the bottom of the trellis, tangled in a thick knot of vines, is a delicate gold chain, a tiny apple charm dangling from its links.

A bracelet I've seen before.

Something in my stomach hardens as I flash back to another apple, this one made of bronze, dancing in a fountain in the middle of the Square. Dancing around the picture of a smiling Lucy Yi, her wrist decorated with an identical golden apple charm bracelet.

I turn the bracelet over in my hand and realize there's an inscription on the back:

GOLDEN APPLE YOUNG INVENTORS CLUB

I look up and down the street, but it's no use. Whoever left me the bracelet and the note is long gone.

"You're not far, though, are you?" I say under my breath.

I look directly across the street at the Peterson house.

"Something tells me you're watching me right now."

CHAPTER 10

I own one suit, which is one more than any person should own. The shirt is stiff, the collar itches my neck, the pants feel grandpa-high up to my chin, and the shoes are so slippery that I could slide off into the next zip code if I'm not careful. Plus, the suit doesn't even fit. I've grown two inches since the last time my parents had it altered, and no matter what I wear it for, I'll only ever remember it as the funeral suit because it's what I wore after my grandma died.

"Five minutes, Narf," Dad says from the other side of my bedroom door, and I can hear his shoes tapping down the hall and back toward my fussing mom.

"Here, let me get that for you," my mom says.

"It's fine, Lu."

"You missed three belt loops," she says.

"I'm trying to expedite my escape from this contraption later on," he says.

"Hon, would you please try to act like a normal human for three hours? These are my colleagues," Mom pleads, and without even seeing him, I know Dad is looking at the ground and nodding. There's enough guilt to waft in my direction, and I look down, too, even though they can't see me. It's for Mom. That's all we need to know about tonight.

* * *

It's obvious that Raven Brooks is proud of their university. The main brick buildings are old, but their trims are freshly painted, their landscaping tightly manicured and closely clipped. Tonight's fund-raiser for a new sciences wing isn't taking place anywhere near the current sciences wing. I guess the organizers figured jars of pickled animal hearts and emergency eye-wash stations didn't create the right atmosphere for a gala. I'm disappointed, though. I'd been hoping to sneak to the library to read the rest of the article I pocketed.

Instead, the fund-raiser takes place in the main library, the centerpiece of the university for good reason. Its ornate carvings and meticulously lined shelves are anything but small town. The crystal stemware and white cloth napkins only add to the formality, leaving little doubt about why I'm wearing a suit, even if it is a size too small.

Mom is across the room wearing the purple dress that Dad likes because Mom feels good in it. She says it hides her lumpy parts, and Dad says he likes her lumpy parts, and that's when I leave the room for fear of throwing up.

But tonight, Mom doesn't look like she's worried about her lumpy parts, or worried about anything really. She looks like she owns the room. Dad is in a corner chasing a goat cheese ball around his plate with a fork and laughing with some donor Mom pointed out to him.

I'm stuffed on goat cheese balls and sparkling grape juice, and I've scoured the shelves—unsuccessfully—for a single book that doesn't look like it would put me in a coma. I'm on my way back from the bathroom, when I see the sign with an arrow pointing downstairs to the archives.

I peek around the corner to make sure my parents are still busy talking to the donors before slipping downstairs. The science library didn't have much in the way of city records, but I'm hopeful the main library will offer more. With my parents distracted, maybe I'll actually have a chance to read a full article this time.

The stacks are piled with newspapers dating back twenty years, when the *Raven Brooks Banner* was simply the *Bulletin*. I learn that Mrs. Bevel, who owns the creepy doll shop, actually has a degree in doll making. (I also learn that doll making is a college degree.) I discover that my street was one of the first streets developed in Raven Brooks, and that our very own not-our-own turquoise house was previously home to a Hollywood stuntwoman. Mrs. Tillman once had to recall a batch of the Surviva cocoa bars that give Aaron and me the farts because the manufacturer found a dead gopher in the chocolate vat. The former mayor of Raven Brooks was impeached for lying about his legislative experience. The llama farm indeed used to have goats.

Overall, I learn that Raven Brooks has always been as boringly strange as it is today.

By the time the *Bulletin* had become the *Raven Brooks Banner*, the news seems to have slowed. Store openings and closings and local weather mainly dominated the headlines. That is, until the Golden Apple factory arrived. Suddenly, Raven Brooks was booming with activity, and the outskirts of town transformed from farmland to houses to serve the needs of the factory workers and their families. And the town grew even more with the explosion in popularity of the Golden Apples, which at first was only a local candy.

"Who would have guessed a local favorite would become a national obsession?" raved one executive of the Golden Apple Corporation in a story dated five years ago.

"I like the chocolate ones best," declared a kid from the same article, pictured with his mouth ringed in said chocolate.

Pretty soon, the factory grew to a storefront, and they began giving tours. Interactive exhibits became lures for out-of-towners, and a new hotel sprung up on Market Street. Then the announcement came—the Golden Apple Corporation would be building a multimillion-dollar theme park right here in Raven Brooks, where it all began.

Every week, at least one story above the fold boasted the progress of the park's construction. I keep reading in morbid fascination. I can't help myself. It's like when magazines publish pictures of Pompeii, with their homes and markets frozen in time, unaware that life would come to a sudden stop.

I thumb through page after page of pictures featuring different parts of the park. It's like there was no other news in town for two years.

I flip the page of one newspaper dated September 14, 1991, which features a crew unwrapping a shiny new carousel, its glitter and bright blues and reds stark against the dirt ground and surrounding trees they hadn't yet cleared.

I set the paper aside and pick up another from the following week. Predictably, there's another Golden Apple Amusement Park story, this one featuring the half-constructed front entrance. There are at least a dozen workers in their safety vests hauling a sign into place. The next week's paper captures a cement mixer pouring concrete, and this time, several small kids gather around the scene, oversized hard hats obscuring all their faces. The next week's article pictures the unraveling of a tarp decorated with shiny gold apples and men and women in suits smiling down at the design.

Finally, I come to the week of August 7, 1992, the headline reading in all capital letters *GOLDEN APPLE AMUSEMENT PARK SET TO OPEN.* A massive crowd of businesspeople in suits and construction workers in coveralls and photographers in vests and local proprietors in red-and-gold polo shirts lines the entrance of the park four rows deep. Each one holds in their extended hand a palm-sized golden apple. Each one smiles brightly, the possibility of the park's success alive in their imaginations. Only one person doesn't hold an apple. Instead, he holds an almost comically large pair of golden scissors over a red ribbon. He wears a black suit with a red-and-gold tie, but I recognize him even out of his argyle sweater.

Mr. Peterson.

It's the caption of the picture, though, that forms a hard pit in my stomach.

Park designed by local engineer Theodore Masters Peterson.

I read it five more times to be sure, but even without the caption, there's no mistaking the mustached face of Aaron's dad.

The following week's paper is almost entirely dedicated to the glory of Golden Apple Amusement Park. The front-page lead story tells of opening-day successes, punctuated by a collage of smiling parents and ecstatic kids, balloons in hand and cotton candy webbed between their fingers.

RAVEN BROOKS BANNER

Local Engineer Brings World-Renowned Talent Home

Peterson has designed parks on six continents! Read on for a sneak peek of his latest undertaking!

Above the fold is a dapper-looking headshot of Mr. Peterson, his carnival mustache twirled at the ends in perfect theme-park-designer character.

Mr. Peterson was—*is*—a sort of genius. A physics whiz, he engineered some of the world's most innovative attractions, bringing new technology and gimmicks to nearly every new park he's designed. There was the vacuum-powered food delivery system at the Alberta Avalanche Park.

"It flies through a tube, just like the tellers use at a bank!" one patron marveled.

There were the robotic vendors at Tokyo's Cherry Blossom Grove.

"I didn't have to wait in line for hours just to buy a key chain!" said another parkgoer.

And as his reputation as an engineer grew, so did his ambitions for his parks. Only instead of looking for business innovations, it seems like Mr. Peterson became more interested in the rides themselves.

At Berlin's Spannend Spaβ Park, he was the first engineer to create a perpetual-motion boomerang ride. Ride operators admitted it could only be stopped by a kill switch on a hidden console.

"I thought I was gonna barf," remarked one rider, whose laughing face betrayed a hint of panic in his picture.

And then there was the Golden Apple Amusement Park, his crowning achievement as an engineer of the world's most exciting attractions.

One could only imagine it had to be spectacular.

The profile reads: *With the park's unprecedented opening-day crowds, we're left wondering what Mr. Peterson has up his sleeve for the big surprise we've come to expect from his parks.*

"You'll just have to wait and see next week," Mr. Peterson is quoted as saying. *"I'll give you a hint, though. Have you noticed there's no roller coaster in this park?"*

The article ends with a reference to the off-limits end of the park, a tarp several stories high, and a showstopping ride that was sure to put Raven Brooks on the map.

I'm not sure if I set the article down so much as push it away under the shelf, appalled at its ignorance of what's to come. I want to scream at the reporter, the smiling patrons in the pictures, and the gleeful, reckless Mr. Peterson, who set such an unimaginable tragedy in motion.

"There you are. Jay, I found him!"

Mom thunders down the stairs looking mostly mad but a little relieved.

I act without thinking, ripping the first few articles from each of the following weeks' newspapers and shoving them into my pocket before tossing the papers to the side.

"You made me sweat all over my favorite dress," she says as she sits down next to the pile of papers I've amassed.

"I got bored," I say as an apology, and the cool thing about Mom is that's all she needs.

"What's all this?" she says, sliding the papers around a little.

"I don't know," I say, which is maybe the most honest thing I've said to my mom in weeks.

She lifts a few of the pictures to the light, and her mouth becomes a thin line. Then, without saying all the obvious stuff about how sad it is to see what everyone thought the park was going to be, she looks at me and says, "I think this move has been the hardest one yet."

There, in the dim light of the library basement in her purple dress, with its little dark rings forming in the armpits, Mom becomes my new favorite person. It's the first time she's ever said what I've never figured out how to say—that after a while, calling so many places "home" just dilutes the word. And she doesn't like it, either.

Dad descends the stairs just as Mom and I are coming back up.

"Hey, Narf," he says, an apology on his face even though he wasn't there for what Mom said. Sometimes, Dad just knows. "I smuggled out some cheesecake for you."

I eat dessert in the car while Mom and Dad rehash the night and laugh about the boring people. I stare out the window at the weird little town of Raven Brooks and realize that its definition of "home" probably changed that awful day at the park a week after it opened. I wonder how many people still feel like they did twenty years ago, or thirty or fifty. Before the day Lucy Yi died.

I wonder how much Aaron thinks his dad is to blame for that.

When I get home, I practically tear off my suit and get into my pajamas, but sleep won't come easily; I have more reading to do.

I pull the crumpled articles from my suit pocket and smooth them across the floorboards of my bedroom.

RAVEN BROOKS BANNER

G.A.A. Park Burns as Investigation Continues

Peterson's past failures resurface — Yi family demands answers!

The first article appears in an issue published a week after the tragedy. It's Mr. Peterson, but his perfectly waxed mustache is less spritely, more . . . pointy. And the picture isn't the only thing unflattering about the new profile in the *Raven Brooks Banner.*

What began as a prayer vigil for young Lucy Yi—the seven-year-old victim of Golden Apple Amusement Park's daredevil roller coaster Rotten Core—ended in a fire that devastated the already infamous attraction. Now investigators are demanding to know why the dangerous roller coaster was allowed to operate before passing certain critical inspections, and angry investors have uncovered troubling details about the man responsible for the park's design.

A knock at my door startles me from the story, and I slide the paper under my bed just in time for Dad to pop his head in to say good night.

"How 'bout that cheesecake, huh?" he says, wiggling his eyebrows.

"It was pretty epic," I say, trying to recall even tasting it.

"Find anything interesting in the library?"

Yes.

"No," I say, shrugging.

"Want me to leave you alone?" he says, a hint of a smile creeping through.

"Kinda."

"Wish I'd just go to bed?" he says, determined to make me crack.

"Well . . ."

"Trying to figure out how to tell me nicely to buzz off?"

"Dad!"

He won. He broke me. He laughs.

"G'night, Narf."

I wait until I hear my parents' bedroom door close before retrieving the article from under my bed.

A resurfaced investigation has raised concerns over the reputation of the world-renowned engineer after reporters unearthed details of a 1987 accident in one of the designer's parks in Melbourne, Australia. What was first thought to be an electrical fire due to faulty wiring in Wallaby Wonderland's Tasmanian Tunnels was later determined to be an accident caused by a critical flaw in the attraction's breaking fail-safe. The accident occurred when an empty car jumped the track, sparking a fire that ignited an exposed patch of insulation, killing four teens, ages thirteen to seventeen.

While investors were found legally responsible, that finding remains disputed as several questions remain about the safety inspections the park failed to undergo prior to its opening.

Said one inspector, "As far as I can tell, no one from my team checked that ride. Not a chance anyone would have given it passing marks without an emergency brake."

The inspector joins a small chorus of objectors—some of them investors accused of trying to deflect blame. But one investor lodged an especially disturbing claim against T. M. Peterson, the park's engineer and mastermind:

"He told me about the mechanics once, about his frustration with its limitation. He said safety features tamped the excitement down. He said emergency brakes put a drag on the speed. The man specifically mentioned emergency brakes!"

But with little evidence and a tragedy half a world away, the Raven Brooks engineer continued his work, bringing what many believe are increasingly unsafe and possibly illegal practices to his park designs—designs that may just be to blame for Lucy Yi's death.

The other front page I borrowed from the library's archives—the issue from two weeks after the accident—avoids the name T. M. Peterson altogether. Instead, it features a window into the life of Lucy Yi, about how she loved her hamster Gerard and played the violin and wanted to be an inventor like Leonardo da Vinci when she grew up.

The picture at the bottom of the article shows Lucy, her fringe of bangs doing little to hide the exuberance in her smile. She's cheek-to-cheek with two other smiling girls, their arms interlocked like sisters, and with a start, I realize that I recognize the face mashed against Lucy's on one side.

It's Mya Peterson.

And like sisters, all three girls in the picture have matching bracelets with little gold charms in the shape of an apple. The picture is captioned: *Mya, Lucy, and Maritza, members of the Golden Apple Young Inventors Club.*

I pull the bracelet that I found beneath the trellis from my desk drawer and hold it up to one of the bracelets pictured on the girls' wrists. It's a perfect match.

CHAPTER 11

I throw a pair of pajamas into my backpack and forgo my toothbrush to make space for the audio manipulator. It's built, and all we need now is to add the prerecorded audio. I survey my bag's contents and decide that pretty much covers all I'll need.

Downstairs, as I slip on my shoes, Dad and Mom watch me a little too closely.

"Excited for your big sleepover?" Dad asks.

"Dad," I say, wincing.

"Sorry, your super grown-up, totally not-a-big-deal hangout where you might wear pajamas and might not sleep."

"That's not better," I say.

"Just remember to brush your teeth," Mom says, and I swear to the Aliens she can see straight through my backpack to my missing toothbrush.

"Uh-huh."

"And say thank you," she says. She's still irked that the Petersons haven't bothered to come by, but to her, "please" and "thank you" are holy words.

"I will," I say.

"And solve the mysteries of the universe," Dad says, and Mom gives him a look.

"What?"

"Are you implying that manners and hygiene are impossible requests of our son?"

"Lu, he's twelve. He's barely human at this age."

I decide to end things before they get ugly. "I'll say thank you," I tell my mom, and she smiles like she's won. "And I'll ponder the meaning of life," I tell Dad, and he gives me a dorky thumbs-up.

As I cross the street, I do ponder, but not about life's meaning. I wonder how in the world I'm going to ask Aaron about everything I read in the old newspapers about Golden Apple Amusement Park, about his dad and Mya. Because there's not even a sliver of a chance that I'll be able to stop myself from asking.

* * *

Mrs. Peterson glides into the room like she's on wheels. I don't even hear her until she's right behind me, a pile of sheets stacked on top of a pillow cradled in her arms. I don't mean to jump; it's just that she surprised me.

"Wow. I know I forgot to put on lipstick today, but exactly how frightening do I look?"

"No, you don't at all. I mean, I just—"

"Nicky, I'm kidding, honey. I have a light step."

"Mom's a teacher, but she danced ballet when she was in college," Mya says as she plunks down on Aaron's bottom bunk. "She even danced at one of Dad's park openings."

"No one invited you, Pariah," Aaron says, nudging Mya off his bed.

"Thank you, Mrs. Peterson," I say, taking the linens from her.

"Hmmm?" she says, her eyes glazed over like she's distracted. "Oh, you can call me Diane, honey," she says, focusing on me long enough to lightly tousle my hair.

"I said stop calling me that," Mya says, shoving Aaron's leg when he pokes her with his toe. "Ow! Your toenails are like knives!"

"Mya Pariah eats farts and papaya," Aaron sings, still poking her.

"Mom!"

Mrs. Peterson—Diane—spreads the sheets across the bottom bunk of Aaron's bed.

"Stop calling your sister a pariah," she says, clearly lost in more pleasant thoughts. She's humming quietly to herself, somehow blocking out the escalating brawl between Aaron and his sister.

"So if you eat farts, does that mean you burp farts, too? Is that why you always smell so bad?"

Mya flushes pink and glances at me.

"I do not smell bad! *Mom!*"

But Diane is already on her way out the door. She's moving slowly, though, almost like she's forgotten where the door is. All at once, Aaron and Mya stop arguing, and a sudden silence blankets the room. In that quiet, I can hear the faint song Mrs. Peterson has been humming to herself. Only now, she's practically whispering it, like she's afraid to scare away the memory attached to the tune.

Mya follows her, still glowing crimson, but she lands a final solid punch on Aaron's bicep on her way out. I watch her leave. Ever since I saw the photo of her, Lucy, and that other girl wearing the golden apple bracelet in the newspaper article, I've been trying to understand what it would mean that the bracelet would find its way into my front yard. I still don't know, but I have a feeling Mya does, which means I'll probably never figure it out. Mya's even less of a sharer than Aaron, if that's possible.

As soon as Mya reaches the stairs at the end of the hall, Aaron closes the bedroom door and waves me to his desk.

He pulls a drawer open, and rather than take anything out of it, he reaches his hand all the way inside until he's shoulder-deep and still reaching. I look at his desk, and it doesn't take me long to determine that what I'm seeing is impossible. Flush against the wall, his desk can't stick out more than a foot and a half.

"What the—?"

Aaron smiles as he struggles to grip whatever hides in his magical desk. Then he gives up and pulls the whole drawer out, exposing its missing back.

We duck down, our heads together, and I understand. There's a hole in his wall. The drawer has a false back.

"You really are a criminal mastermind," I say, and Aaron chuckles. Then he hauls out his treasure.

It's a box full of junk of the very best kind: There're dismantled motors and remote-control cars, parts of an old toaster, some speaker wire, clamps and locks, keys to nowhere, a discarded keyboard, a phone without its faceplate, and at least three broken calculators.

It's a gadget head's bounty.

"Holy Aliens, Aaron," I say, and he smiles in a way that I haven't seen. I think this is what pride looks like on Aaron. From one weirdo to another, I know how elusive pride can be.

"It's all stuff I collected from the factory before you moved here. I wanted to make something out of it, except I don't know how." He looks at me. "Think you can use any of the parts for your audio synthesizer?"

"The synthesizer!" I can't believe I almost forgot. Reaching for my bag, I pull out the finished product, and as quickly as Aaron's face lights up, it dims again, and I realize that maybe he wanted to help me finish it.

"It's not ready yet," I hurry to explain, and some of the light returns to Aaron's face.

"No?"

I shake my head slowly and explain. "We still need the recording."

He smiles so wide, I think his face might split apart.

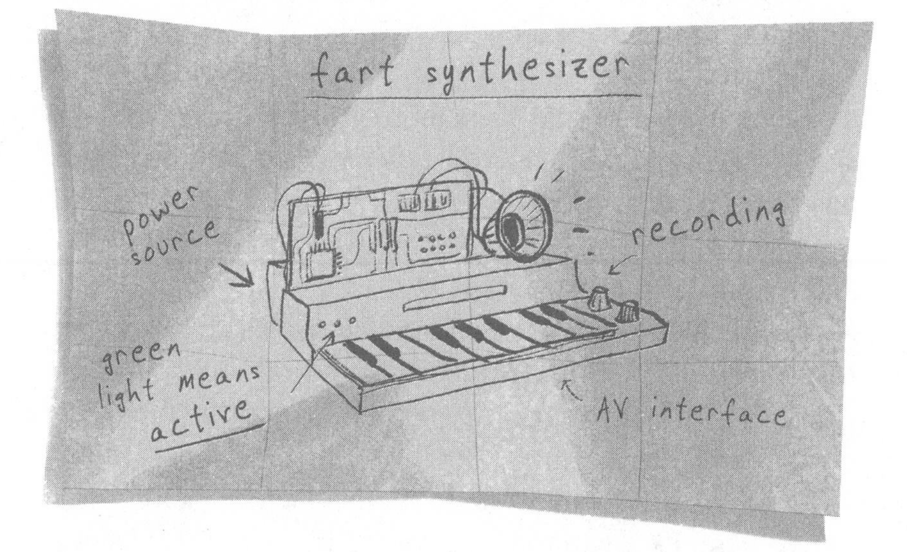

An hour later, stuffed on Surviva bars and bloated to the point of bursting, Aaron and I are a mess. I'm laughing so hard, I can barely hold the microphone to the, er, audio source. Every time Aaron lets one rip, we fall apart, rolling across his floor like beetles on our backs.

It takes everything in me to gather myself, and I plaster on my most serious face, placing a hand on Aaron's shoulder.

"Fine, sir," I say. "I daresay that was your best work yet."

He matches my seriousness, but only for a second, and then we both break.

"Boys," Mrs. Peterson says, peeking in the doorway. "Are you planning to come down for pizza at any point tonight or—sweet Mary, what is that smell?"

I laugh so hard my sides pinch. Aaron swipes the tears from his eyes.

"Sorry, Mom," he says. "We're, uh—"

"Performing an experiment," I say.

"Creating art," he says over me. Then we bust up all over again.

"Well, whatever you're doing, open a window, for Pete's sake," Mrs. Peterson says. "That's toxic."

Aaron farts, this time accidentally, and I have to bury my face in the bottom bunk to keep myself from laughing to death—or suffocating. Either one is equally plausible.

Once we've calmed down enough to choose a series of Aaron's choicest farts for the synthesizer, we're suddenly at a loss for things to do. It's late, but neither of us is tired. Still, maybe out of habit or boredom, we pull on pajamas and take to our bunks, Aaron on the top bunk, me staring at the slats from the bottom.

It's not the right time, because no time is the right time,

but somehow it seems more possible to talk to Aaron about his dad when I only have to stare at the mattress above me and not at his face.

"So, I gotta ask," I say, trying to sound casual.

"No, I don't believe in aliens," Aaron says.

"Wait, what?"

"Sorry, man. I know it's your . . . I dunno, religion or whatever," he says.

"It's not my religion." Then I catch myself. Pushing my shock aside (seriously, how can he not believe in aliens?—the proof is overwhelming), I try again to bring up the most awkward conversation ever.

"So, what's up with your dad anyway?"

The silence that follows is painful. I only have myself to blame; it was perhaps history's worst segue.

"What do you mean?" Aaron asks, but he's quiet, and his voice doesn't ask, *What do you mean?* as much as, *How much do you know?*

"I mean, he's pretty . . . intense . . ." I say. This is excruciating. At this rate, it's going to take me a week to work up the courage to ask him what I really want to ask him—if Aaron knows his dad is suspected of purposely making rides unsafe. Ugh, even *thinking* it sounds absurd. Still, I can't shake the feeling he wants me to ask him. Why else would he "accidentally" bring me by Golden Apple Amusement Park?

Aaron shifts in his bunk overhead, and I hold as still as I can so I don't miss a word.

"Just ask me what you want to ask me," he says, and suddenly he does sound tired. He sounds like he hasn't slept in years. It's the old Aaron again, the one I encountered on our first few times hanging out. He's old beyond his years, burdened by something unseen.

I've aged him. I weighed him down by bringing up the past—a past he has to know about. Of course he has to know about it.

"Why did you want me to know about the park?" I ask, and he's quiet for so long, I think maybe he's decided to stop talking to me for the rest of the night.

Then, after a long while, he says, "He was a genius, you know. Like, a real, Einstein-level genius."

I don't say anything because I *do* know that. And I don't want to stop him talking now that he's finally started up again.

"I'm not happy Lucy Yi died," he says, and this takes me off guard because of course he's not. Who would ever be happy about something like that? Then I remember something else he said to me in this very room, something he said like a confession, even though I didn't know it at the time.

What does *make a person bad, then?*

Being happy when bad things happen.

"But he stopped after that," Aaron said, and I understand now.

The accident that killed Lucy also killed Mr. Peterson's career, a career that was becoming increasingly reckless with every new venture.

Then Aaron really does stop talking. Before long, I hear the slow, even breath of his slumber above me. The weight on him has disappeared, at least for now. But it isn't actually gone. The weight has shifted to me, and I wonder how I'll ever fall asleep like him.

I lie awake for what feels like an eternity, staring at the slats above my bunk, thinking about how long Aaron's blamed himself for simply feeling relieved.

Relief in the form of Lucy Yi's death.

* * *

When I wake up, the only light in the room emanates from the recording light on the audio simulator. Aaron is still in the top bunk. His snoring is the only clear indication he's even alive. I try to remember the last time I've slept that soundly.

Except he's not exactly peaceful. He's twitching—hard—and if I listen closely enough between bouts of snoring, I can hear him begging to the things of his nightmares—"no" and "don't" and "please."

I lie there for a moment, trying to figure out what exactly it was that woke me up. I was dreaming again, but this dream didn't start in the cart, or in the grocery store at all. This one started in a tunnel. It closed in on me, edging closer and closer to my shoulders and the top of my head until I began to sink. I dropped to the bottom of something deep and dark, so dark I wasn't sure my eyes were even open. And while I don't remember much after that, I do remember the voice that hissed to me across that deep, dark expanse. I remember the chilling words it whispered to me:

Find me.

And then I woke up. But it wasn't the voice from my dream that woke me. It was a sound.

But like the voice from my dream, the sound that woke me is long gone, and in its place is thirst.

Between the Surviva bars and the pizza we did eventually sneak downstairs to eat, my mouth is a desert, and as I stare at the bunk above me where Aaron twitches away, I know there's no way I'm going back to sleep until I can get something to drink.

Snatching a flashlight from the pile of orphaned electronics on Aaron's floor, I creep down the hall, taking care to avoid as many squeaky floorboards as I can, but Aaron's house is full of them. Mya's door is shut tight, but Mr. and Mrs. Peterson's door stands open a crack, and I can barely make out the rustle of sheets as I sneak by.

Just find the kitchen, get a drink, and go back to bed, I tell myself. There's something weird about sneaking around your friend's house when everyone else is asleep. When you're awake, you're a guest. But when the rest of the house sleeps, it's hard not to feel like an intruder.

The thought of Mr. Peterson mistaking me for a home invader is enough to propel me down the stairs, and even though I know I made too much noise, at least I'm past the worst part now that I'm downstairs.

Except I'm not past the worst part because suddenly I'm lost. I hold the flashlight up, disbelieving that I could *actually* have lost my way from the stairs to the kitchen. But I really have. The doorway to the kitchen should be right in front of me, shouldn't it? I walk forward, not believing what the flashlight is showing me. Yet there it is, a wall where there should be a kitchen. I look to my right, but the living room isn't there, either. In fact, all that's in front of me is a long hallway.

I stop cold, the contents of my anxious thoughts creeping into my waking life. I shake it off, though, and remind myself that I'm just tired and thirsty, and I haven't ever seen this house at night. It's kind of a maze even in the daytime, so I must have taken a wrong turn somewhere between the upstairs hallway and the stairs leading here.

I keep walking, still hopeful that I'll find the kitchen just a little farther ahead. I don't, though. Instead, I find myself surrounded by closed doors, each boasting a slightly different doorknob and keyhole.

"What—?"

I'm just about to turn around and retrace my steps back up the stairs when I hear a sound I'd hoped to never hear again from this house—ice-cream-truck music.

The melody winds up, then down again, then goes silent and repeats the pattern. I step lightly across the floor of the hallway, pressing my ear against each door I pass. Yet none of them seems to hide the source of the sound.

Then the music stops. I wait to see if it returns, but all that greets me are the creaks and groans of someone else's home. I've lived in enough houses that belong to other people to not be freaked out by those sounds. Still, there was something about that—

Thud.

I stop cold. Straining, I wait to hear it again. I don't have to wait long.

Thud.

This time closer. This time with a dragging sound that follows. Then another thud.

There's no mistaking the sound now. It's footsteps. Footsteps that aren't moving quite right.

I swallow, but I can't wet my dry throat. I want to turn around and go back up the stairs, but now I'm not entirely certain the sound was coming from up ahead. The hallway is playing tricks on my ears, and the thudding and dragging now sounds like maybe it's coming from behind me.

A groggy Mr. Peterson creeping up behind what he thinks is an intruder.

A sleepwalking Aaron fumbling through his house.

An *actual* intruder.

None of the possibilities slow my thumping heart, and why didn't I just get some water from the bathroom upstairs?

The thudding and dragging speed up, and all at once, I understand why it's getting louder: It's moving toward me.

I turn to open the door behind me, no longer trying to figure out where the sound is coming from. All I can think of is hiding until it passes. But the doorknob won't budge. I try one farther down the hall, but it's locked, too. The thudding is louder still, and I try another door. Mercifully, this one opens, and I fall through it, closing the door behind me a little too hard. I wince at the sound, then wait to see if the footsteps pass.

Suddenly, I don't hear them anymore. I press my ear to the door, but it's as though there was never any noise in the first place. No music. No footsteps. No creaks or groans in the walls or pipes.

My flashlight is trained to a single spot on the floor, and only now do I realize I'm standing on a well-worn area rug—the kind you'd find in the sitting room of some rich old lady's house. Like maybe it was nice a long time ago, but now it just looks like it's trying to hide something worse underneath.

I swing my flashlight across the room and find it cluttered with so much furniture, I can hardly see the walls that frame the space. There are bureaus and bookshelves, glass cases protecting plaques framed in wood and statuettes carved from crystal. I move closer and see Mr. Peterson's name etched into every single one, each praising him for a different accomplishment.

One of the glass cases abuts a massive wooden desk that takes up a fourth of the room, and so much paperwork clutters the desk, even the imposing piece of furniture looks like it might buckle under the weight.

I train the light on the papers, spread haphazardly across the surface, trying to make sense of a room that at one time must have served as an office to Mr. Peterson.

There are large curled blueprints paperweighted at their corners, with measurements and precise notations penciled beside each line and curve. Some of the names I recognize from old newspaper articles: the Bell Tower, the Dead Weight, the Dragon's Lair—the most dangerous thrill rides from Mr. Peterson's parks across the world. There are some I don't recognize: the Inverted Cyclone, the Whip—whose curves and lines cover the entire space of the blueprint.

There's one blueprint that isn't done, that doesn't even have a name, but it spirals to the edges of the paper at angles that seem to defy gravity. A smattering of red Xs mark areas on the design like some kind of treasure map, only instead of signaling treasure, the Xs have words beside them like *Access 1*, *Egress 2*, and *Hatch 3*.

My mind is trying to keep up, but disorientation and fear have given way to exhaustion, and I'm distracted by the need for water and sleep.

I've just about resolved to ask Aaron about the room and the blueprints tomorrow morning when the beam of my flashlight lands on a filing cabinet shoved against the wall beside the desk. It's packed so fully, the drawers are spilling out their contents, with one fat file seemingly dominating the drawer. In thick black marker, the file label reads *Golden Apple Amusement Park*.

My heartbeat quickens, and I grab for the file without thinking. Common sense should have made me rethink snooping in Mr. Peterson's study, but I seem to have lost common sense as I lost my way in this winding house.

I try pulling the file from the drawer, but it's wedged in too tightly. Instead, all I manage is to dislodge a couple of papers, sending another few fluttering to the floor to join an already growing pile of spilled contents.

The first piece of paper is a letter printed on thick stationery, with the kind of letterhead that embosses the paper.

From the Offices of Lin, Gruber & Fonseca

Dear Mr. Peterson:

It is with prejudice that we inform you we are disinclined to pursue charges against you, your business holdings, and any assets thereby affected by said holdings. While we feel a significant portion of the liability of the death of our client's daughter lies in your hands, given the State court's findings placing sole responsibility on the Golden Apple Corporation, our client has elected not to pursue civil damages finding you criminally responsible in the death of Lucy Yi.

While we reserve the right to reengage in proceedings at a later date, consider this letter official notice that we are discontinuing pursuit of charges against you, one Theodore Masters Peterson.

Sincerely,

Fonseca

I blink at the letter and translate the legal jargon as best as I can. Their client's daughter was Lucy Yi. It must have been Lucy's parents suing Mr. Peterson for their daughter's death. But the state found the Golden Apple Corporation responsible, not Mr. Peterson, which means Mr. Peterson probably would have been absolved in civil court, too. I picture my parents in that same situation, stone-faced in a courtroom while some faceless company is named as my killer. I wonder how it feels to hurt that badly, to not get an apology, to not be able to look anyone in the eye and say, "You're the reason I don't make jokes anymore or eat cake or go to parks because there are too many kids there who'll remind me of the one I don't have anymore." I wonder how it feels to be robbed like that, again and again.

I wonder how it feels to know your dad was the real robber.

I accidentally step on the pile of papers I've contributed to on the floor. In the shadows of the study, they look like grainy photographs of a forest, a construction site, a group of people crowded around a worktable. But when I pick them up and lay them across the desk, the beam from my flashlight reveals something unexpected.

The first picture is a photocopy of a newspaper article:

Ground Breaks on Hometown Landmark: Construction Begins on Buzzed-About Golden Apple Amusement Park.

Below the headline is a thick grove of trees, a bulldozer,

and a team of workers with chain saws ready to clear the land. Mr. Peterson is in the foreground, construction hat high on his head, mustache curled to match his smile. But in the background, nearly out of frame, is a stooped figure lurking by one of the trees. I likely wouldn't have noticed him at all if not for the red ink encircling his figure, the pen retracing the circle so many times the page is torn.

I might not have noticed it at all, but now that I do, there's no mistaking who it is. Blurry and marred in red ink, it's Aaron. He's younger—five years younger if it's at the start of the construction—but it's Aaron, and while he's blurry, it's hard to deny that his pose implies he's hiding.

I push that page aside and find another photocopy of an article:

Ahead of Schedule! Pressure Mounts for Golden Apple Amusement Park to Open by Summer.

In this picture, Mr. Peterson points to a crane swinging a beam across the framework of what was to become the base of the fun house, judging by the gaping mouth surrounding the beginnings of a track. All eyes are on Mr. Peterson in the picture, including the crouched boy, circled in red, peeking out from the fun house framing.

The next article is dominated by an entire crew of men in vests and hard hats staring upward at a structure so tall, it doesn't fit in the frame, which makes it more noticeable that one head stares straight ahead, or rather at

BROOKS BANNER
PETERSON BREAKS GROUND!!!
AHEAD
Pressure Moun

ULE!
Summer
RAVEN BROOKS BANNER
Golden Apple Amusement Park Underway!!!
OMEN

Mr. Peterson standing at the front of the group. Aaron is once again encircled in red ink, hanging back by a pile of iron rods.

Page after page shows Aaron nearly out of frame, ousted from his hiding place by the red pen's wielder. I look around at the rest of the office, its hulking furniture casting distorted shadows across the framed pictures of the Peterson family. It strikes me that this is the only room in the entire house where I've seen any family photos at all. But when I examine the pictures closer, I see that they've also been marred by red ink. The placid, smiling faces of Mrs. Peterson and Mya grace most of the pictures, as does Mr. Peterson's. The only unsmiling face is Aaron's.

And as the Peterson family ages, their smiles turn from placid to pinched, and Aaron's face disappears altogether behind the scribble of that angry red pen. Only one picture offers more than a scribble—what appears to be the last family portrait taken of the Petersons, judging by their ages. Beside the etched-away face of Aaron is what I first read as his name. But when I look closer, I see that the word isn't "AARON."

It's "OMEN."

I drop the flashlight and the room goes black. I stand in place, trembling on a squeaky floorboard it's too late to avoid. Then, from somewhere in the dark, I hear the slow creak of a door swinging open.

I was so engrossed in the pictures, I didn't even hear the footsteps return.

The thump, the drag, the labored movement of whatever has emerged into the room, is so close that I can hear breathing I know isn't mine.

Run. *Run!*

But my stupid feet are stuck.

I want to be dreaming. Please let me be dreaming.

But I'm not. I know I'm not.

The breathing grows louder, like an animal preparing to pounce. I hold perfectly still, my only defense in the pitch-black of the room. But whoever is here knows I'm here. Floorboards moan under the weight of feet that methodically make their way toward me. They step to the glass case, rattling the awards on their shelves. They step to the desk, with its papers exposed to my prying eyes. They step to the filing cabinet, its papers still protruding from the drawer.

They step so close to me that I can feel that hot, menacing breath on the back of my neck. In its exhale, I hear my name.

"Nicholas," the voice says. "You shouldn't be here."

A soft glow illuminates the floor and the flashlight at my feet. Looming over me is an impossibly long shadow.

I turn because I don't know what else to do. I can't run. I can't hide. All I can do is face the shadow.

Heat hits my face and temporarily blinds me, and when my eyesight returns, the first thing I make out is argyle.

I tilt my head to reach the top of Mr. Peterson's face, and I don't like what I see. His eyes, darkened and distorted by the flame of the candle he holds, are barely visible. Below his eyes are the flaring nostrils of a man whose house I should not be wandering without permission, whose private office I should absolutely not be rummaging through. His thick mustache curls upward mockingly, belying the frown that's only barely visible underneath.

I look down at my bare feet again, terrified and embarrassed, which is the only reason I notice that Mr. Peterson's shoes are on.

In the middle of the night.

I look up again, taking in his pants and his argyle sweater. I'm in my pajamas, but Mr. Peterson is fully clothed.

I struggle for answers to questions I think he might ask, but he doesn't ask anything. In fact, he hasn't said another word since I turned around to face him. He's just . . . staring.

I watch the light from his candle flicker and sway in the draft of the house, but Mr. Peterson holds it perfectly still. That's how I notice his hands, smeared and coated in something thick and dark.

My eyes travel upward, and I don't know if I'm expecting an explanation for why he's here, what's on his hands, why he's up so late—or if he's expecting an explanation from me—but what I'm not expecting is that smile. That horrible, out-of-place, unhappy smile that's suddenly crept out from under his mustache and spread across his face.

Then he starts to laugh. It's a low rumble from his gut at first, but soon it travels through his chest and his throat and out of his mouth, and the light, airy giggle is so vastly different from the growl it started as, I am all at once aware of how much of the room he takes up. His shoulders are broad enough to equal twice my width. I can barely see the doorway behind him.

And all I want is that doorway.

Then, as suddenly as his horrifying laughter started, it stops, and he holds the silence between us with a grasp as tight as that on his candle. He leans down, inches from my face, and meets my eyes.

"Nighty night, Nicky," he says, and with a single puff, he blows out the candle and steps aside.

I sprint out of the room and find the stairs, running on feet I can't even feel anymore. I run past the hallway I was so desperate to traverse quietly moments ago. In Aaron's room, I swing the door shut behind me, locking it against what lurks in the darkness. I look to the top bunk where Aaron sleeps, certain the commotion woke him, but he doesn't even snore anymore. He lies still, his face obscured by the comforter, and I wait for a second to see if he's actually awake behind there.

When only silence greets me, I'm left with the sound of my heart pounding away in my ears, my teeth chattering in violent rhythm as I fight to calm myself. Then, once I'm finally still, I prop my pillow against the wall and watch the door from the bottom bunk, flinching every time the wood of the old house pops or settles.

I've forgotten the drawer full of possibilities.

I've forgotten the water I never drank.

I've forgotten the excitement I had about finally making a friend as strange as me.

All I remember is the music in the basement. Photo after photo of Aaron's circled image. The grime on Mr. Peterson's hands.

And that mad, mad smile that grew from a face that's forgotten joy.

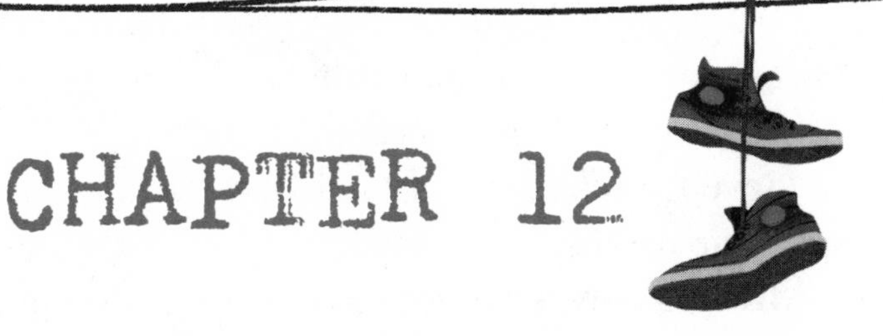

CHAPTER 12

I throw my gray hoodie on over my backpack, but I should have known Dad would see it anyway.

"Getting a head start on studying, Narf?" he says, flicking a finger toward my hunchback.

"Never too early," I say, then shrug. It's the best antidote to his inquiries, a vague response with a shrug. He shakes his head and goes back to whisking whatever is bubbling on the stove. I can barely see the top of Mom's head under all the steam emanating from dinner. She doesn't seem to notice, though. She's onto something.

"Be safe," she says without looking up, before she knows where I'm going.

"Going to Aaron's," I say, even though I think I could have gotten away with saying nothing at all.

"You're spending an awful lot of time over there," Dad says, whisking so hard he's doing a little dance from the hips down. "Whatever happened to Miguel's son, Enzo?"

"The Petersons don't mind," I say, avoiding the topic of Enzo altogether.

"Lu, we really should have them over," he says, but Mom

raises her hand to stop him, still not looking up from whatever formula has her rapt attention.

"Seven weeks," she says, like we're supposed to know what she means.

Miraculously, Dad *does* know what she means. "Honey, come on."

"Nope," she says, and we all know it's the end of the conversation. Whatever she says next is just meant to educate us, not to debate. "Seven weeks and no invitation over. They don't want to know us; we don't need to know them."

She actually means a lot more than she says. We've lived in enough places to understand the weight under a non-invite, or a failure to say hello, or the silence that follows when Dad introduces "Lu, my wife," or Mom points to, "Jay, my husband." Maybe it's because "Lu, my wife," has at times been described as abrasive, or "Jay, my husband," has had to call far too many newspapers "his" newspaper to be considered a real newsman. Maybe it's because "the Roth family" is a Jewish one, or maybe it's because our house is older, or our cereal is off-brand, or our license plates are from another state, or our accents don't quite match this side of the country. What we know by now is that "We don't need to know them" is Mom's way of protecting us from what people say when they're trying to be polite, or what they *don't* say when they're trying not to be rude.

This isn't the conversation I want to have tonight, though. Not any night really, but especially not tonight. I just want to get out the door before I give myself away.

"I'll talk to them, okay?" I say, and Mom makes a *pssht* sound.

"Don't bother," she says, but she says it with a little singsongy voice so I can tell she's not too upset. Not at the moment, anyway. She's deep in the throes of her research now. I can tell by the way she keeps cracking her knuckles.

"Don't be too late," Dad says, but he's smiling at Mom like he always does. My backpack and the amount of time I spend across the street are already distant memories.

The Petersons' front door is open a crack, and I look around for anyone in the yard. It's empty, though. In fact, the whole house seems quiet.

I knock softly on the door before opening it a little wider. "Hello? Aaron? Anyone there?" Then, a little softer, "Mr. Peterson?"

I've seen less and less of Aaron's dad lately, a development I couldn't be happier about after our encounter in his study I still haven't been able to find again, even in the daytime, not that I'd want to. Stranger than that, though, is the way no one else in the family seems to bring up his increasing absence. It's like he's sort of just . . . fading away.

I hover by the door for a minute before pulling out Aaron's note.

My house at 5:00.

I check my watch. It's 5:03.

Normally I'm not such a stickler for time, but I'm more nervous for this prank than I've been about the others. Maybe it's because I haven't had an opportunity to test the synthesizer with another audio system. Maybe it's because I've been on edge ever since that night at Aaron's. I tried asking Aaron about it in the morning, but I don't really know what it was I saw. Whatever it was, one thing was clear: Mr. Peterson sees something in Aaron, and judging by Aaron's presence in all those pictures, he sees something in his dad, too.

What that is, I can barely begin to guess, but it has something to do with Golden Apple Amusement Park.

I look at my watch again. 5:05.

"Mrs. Peterson?" I try again, then knock a little louder on the open door. "Uh . . . I mean Diane?"

This is definitely an intrusion. Aaron and I might have had solid plans, but that plan didn't include me strolling through his house when no one's here. The door is open, though. Maybe Aaron meant for me to come in.

I'm almost to the kitchen before it dawns on me that something could be wrong.

I turn in every direction—the kitchen, the stairway, the three hallways that lead to different corners of the house, then back to the open front door.

"Okay, I've seen all I need to see," I whisper, resolved to give Aaron a hard time later about chickening out.

I turn back toward the door and straight into the broad chest of a towering Mr. Peterson.

"Aaron's not here."

I back up so fast I bump into the couch, nearly falling over it.

"The door was open," I say stupidly.

Mr. Peterson doesn't say anything. He just looks at me. No, that's not right. He looks *through* me. I bet he could see what I had for lunch. Not for long, though, because I'm about to lose it.

"I . . . uh . . . I called for—"

"Aaron's not here," he says again, and this time it sounds a lot more like *Get out of my house before I melt you into a human pile of wax with my death-ray eyes*.

"Right. Okay. Absolutely. I was just on my way out."

I babble all the way to the door, closing it so fast that I catch my heel and scrape the skin, but I hardly feel the sting as I skitter across the street, eyes over my shoulder, waiting for Mr. Peterson to come lumbering through the door and lunging toward me. I'm to the sidewalk when I allow myself to run through what I saw—Mr. Peterson was in his usual argyle sweater, but something was very wrong. His mustache was curled so crisply that the tips practically touched his eyebrows. He had that gunk on his hands again, but this time, he'd smeared it on his pants, too. His hair was a mess, and from the smell of him, I'd guess he hadn't showered in a few days. And there was something else, something truly unsettling.

He looked scared. No, scratch that. He looked *terrified.*

"Where've you been?"

I spin hard enough that this time, I do feel the sting of my heel. I buckle under the burn and look down to see that I've started bleeding through my sock and all over the back of my Vans.

When I look up, Aaron is leaning against the streetlight looking bored.

"What do you mean 'Where have *I* been?' Where have *you* been?" I ask, and it comes out a little angrier than I mean for it to, but my shoes. These are actual Vans, not knockoffs. I was so lucky to get them for my birthday last year—Dad got a nice bonus for once. But now they've got blood on them, and why the heck wasn't Aaron where he said he'd be?

"Whoa, whoa," he says, putting his hands up in surrender. "I didn't realize the plan was firm."

"Seriously?" I say, folding the heel of the canvas under my foot so I can minimize the damage.

"Jeez, sorry," he says, and it's not enough. I'm mad at him for acting like it's no big deal. Maybe it's more than that. Maybe I'm mad that the more I think I understand Aaron, the more mysterious his whole life seems.

"Hey," he says, this time looking genuinely concerned. "This is gonna be epic." I back down because he's not wrong. This *is* going to be epic. The only thing that's gotten me through trips to the natural grocer with my mom and Mrs. Tillman's phony smiles and condescension is the thought of showing people what her fake enlightenment really is—a bunch of farts disguised to sound like caring. She isn't Zen. She's just plain old greedy.

I start off ahead of Aaron, still not totally over my frustration until he says, "Your Vans look cooler like that."

Then I'm okay. Because he knew.

I shift my backpack to my other shoulder, and we take side streets to the natural grocer. We tell each other it's so we won't be seen, but really I think it's because that's the long way, and maybe I'm not the only one who's more nervous for this prank.

"You remember the plan, right?" I say.

"Dude, it's *my* plan. Of course I remember it."

We agreed that I would be the one to distract Mrs. Tillman while Aaron hooks up the synthesizer. I should be handling the install, but it's more believable that I would be looking for a birthday gift for my mom; Mrs. Peterson has already made her opinion of Mrs. Tillman's store pretty known.

We're almost to the store now. We wait for the rush-hour traffic of Sixth Street to clear, then Frogger our way through the straggling cars and parked vans outside of the natural grocer, hoping the loaded backpack isn't a dead giveaway.

"Remember to disable the primary audio outlet first," I say to Aaron.

"I know."

"And you know to start the volume super low, right?"

"Right. Super low."

"Because the synthesizer is three times as amplified as a normal audio system."

"Uh-huh," he says.

"So if you don't start it low—"

"Dude, calm down," Aaron says.

"You do realize we're toast if we get caught," I say. "More than with Farmer Llama. Like, burnt-to-a-crisp toast. Like, butt-on-fire toast."

"Yeah, I get it. Flames and roasted nuts and all that," Aaron says, but somehow, I feel unconvinced.

The little bell above the door announces our arrival at the natural grocer. Smoothly, Aaron slips the backpack from my shoulder and makes his way to the back of the store, snaking through the aisles with the more obscure products. Mrs. Tillman interrupts her own conversation with a customer and takes a moment to eye me. She didn't see Aaron.

When she's done extolling the benefits of wheatgrass to a skeptical-looking man, she turns her full attention to me.

"Hello . . ."

"Nicky," I remind her, even though every time I've been in here with my mom, she's reminded Mrs. Tillman that my name isn't Mikey.

"Right. And what brings you in today?"

"I'm, uh, looking for a birthday gift for my mom," I say, just like Aaron and I rehearsed.

"Oh!" Mrs. Tillman looks shocked, and I can feel myself getting defensive already.

"Do you have anything you could recommend?" I ask, pretending to look around at the shelves but really searching for Aaron. I see his head bobbing down the last aisle by the stairs to the office. The intercom is by the little window that looks out over the whole store from the loft.

"For your mother, you say?" Mrs. Tillman says, and a weird little smile creeps across her face.

"Yeah. My mom," I say, pointedly, my full focus back on

Mrs. Tillman because now I know what she's getting at. "Is there something wrong with that?"

"No, no," Mrs. Tillman says, and she's terrible at faking sincerity. "I just didn't think she was—"

"That she was what?" I can feel my face getting hot.

"Well, you know, the products I sell are for people who have reached a certain level of . . . enlightenment."

"She has a PhD," I say.

Mrs. Tillman smiles again. "What I mean is, one needs to possess more than academic intelligence," she explains like she's doing me a favor. Like there's no way I could possibly understand.

I turn away so she can't see how red my face is getting, or how my eyes are starting to feel wet. Then, as I blink the burning from my eyes, I see Aaron's face in the office window above. He's smiling and giving me a thumbs-up, and I think I've never felt more powerful in my whole life.

I turn back to Mrs. Tillman, voice steady.

"I'll just look around. You've got customers," I say, nodding to the small line that's formed in the time since she's been talking to me. There's the man with the wheatgrass and a woman with twin kindergartners playing jump rope with the coiled aisle separators.

Mrs. Tillman leaves without excusing herself and scolds the kids for playing on the rope before reaching down to grab the microphone under the register.

"Cashier assistance" is what her mouth forms, but all that comes over the loudspeaker is the sound of Aaron's juiciest, loudest, most earthshattering fart we could record after a night of Surviva bars and two hearts bent on class warfare.

A collective silence follows as we all process what just happened. The kindergartners are the ones to break first.

"Mommy, she tooted!" says the girl, laughing riotously.

"Say excuse me," the little boy admonishes.

Color drains from Mrs. Tillman's face as she starts to deny it, but her finger is still on the microphone's button, and instead of "I did not," her mouth farts again.

The twins squeal and clap at the performance while the mother tries to settle them. I look at the man at the front of the line.

"Must be the wheatgrass," I say, and he sets it down so fast, the canister tips over and rolls down the aisle.

I look up at the office, but I don't see Aaron anymore.

Mrs. Tillman pursues the wheatgrass down the aisle as the mother loses control of the twins altogether.

"Let me try!" says the boy, who reaches the microphone first.

He presses the button and releases another echoing fart, and the kids squeal and trade places.

"Mommy!" the little girl screams into the microphone, sending flatulence thundering across the store. A few more people I didn't even know were in the store pop their heads up from the aisles like groundhogs, looking mortified, like they were the ones who'd let it rip. Then they turn their silent judgment on Mrs. Tillman, who's still chasing the can of wheatgrass down the far aisle.

Right toward the stairs to the office.

I hear her before I see Aaron.

"You!" she says, and another fart tears through the store. The kindergartners have teamed up now, pressing their mouths against the microphone at the same time.

The speakers begin to crackle, and the elation I felt for one glorious minute turns to horror as I realize that the speakers are getting ready to blow. Aaron must have turned the volume up too far.

"I knew you two were up to something! You may have pulled one over on Betty Bevel, but not me. Not this enlightened soul!" Mrs. Tillman shrieks, chasing Aaron up the aisle, barely sidestepping the canister of wheatgrass.

"Busted," Aaron hisses as he flies past me.

"Stop right there!" Mrs. Tillman screams, lunging after Aaron, but now I'm ahead of him, trying to pry the kindergartners off the microphone before they blow the speakers out.

"Wait your turn!" one of them says while the other bites my hand.

"Ah!" I pull my hand back just as the mother yanks him off of me, but the little girl is still at the microphone, scream-farting into the microphone as the speakers pop and crack.

Aaron jumps on top of the checkout counter to escape Mrs. Tillman's wrath, but it's not him she's reaching for. Instead, she reaches under the counter and slams her hand on a hidden button. Alarm bells sound, and red lights flash, and suddenly a mesh gate closes over both entrances of the store.

I look at Aaron, and his wide eyes confirm what I really wanted him to deny—we're cooked.

Between the synthesizer and the alarm, the speakers buckle under the pressure, emitting one earsplitting pop before dying under a fizzle of static. Magically, the alarm still blares from a backup system. A tap at the door catches Mrs. Tillman's attention, and she rushes to let the guest in.

A tired-looking uniformed officer strolls in, hands over his ears, and surveys the store for what went wrong.

"These boys! Arrest these boys!" Mrs. Tillman screams, but the officer refuses to uncover his ears.

"Marcia, the siren, please?"

He nods to the register, evidently aware that Mrs. Tillman is paranoid enough to have installed a full-blown Fort Knox-level alarm system in her stupid store.

She hurries to the counter and types in a code, silencing the siren and stopping the red lights from flashing.

The officer takes a slow scan of the now-silent store,

meeting the gaze of every shocked face until he comes to Mrs. Tillman, who has been waiting impatiently to speak, tapping her fingers on the countertop. The officer takes his wire-framed glasses off, drags his palm down his face, then slowly puts his glasses on again.

"Go on and tell me what happened, Marcia."

"I think it's obvious, Keith," she says, and it strikes me that she and the officer are on a first-name basis, which at first grosses me out because I think maybe they're dating or something, but taking one more look at Officer Keith, it's clear there's someone else in Raven Brooks who dislikes Mrs. Tillman as much as Aaron and I.

"Well, then pretend like it's not clear to all of us," he says.

"That lady farted," says the boy who bit my hand.

"I did not—"

"It was the wheatgrass," says the man at the front of the line.

"Nope. Surviva bars," Aaron says, and the twins dissolve into giggles. Aaron starts to laugh, too, and I can't believe it. We're up to our eyeballs in trouble, and he's laughing like a kindergartner?

"It wasn't—Oh, for heaven's sake," says Mrs. Tillman. "These, *boys*, did something to my intercom system!"

She says "boys" like she doesn't actually believe we're *boys*. Urchins, maybe. Or aliens. Or meat products. Officer Keith looks between me and Aaron, then settles on me.

"Is that true, young man? Did you vandalize Mrs. Tillman's intercom?"

"I, uh—it's more like—it wasn't . . ."

"I did it."

The entire store turns to Aaron, and I'm too shocked to say anything for a moment.

"You did what, exactly?" asks Officer Keith.

"I blew out her speakers. I was the one. It was all me," he says. "I guess the gas made me do it."

"That's not true," I say, trying to understand why Aaron would take the fall, why he's making so light of it.

"It *is* true," he says calmly, like he's lied a thousand times before.

"No, it's not. Aaron, what are you—?"

"It was both of them!" Mrs. Tillman shrieks, and Officer Keith puts his hands up.

"Okay, okay, I think I've got a clear enough picture of what's going on," he says, looking back at the boy who accused Mrs. Tillman of farting.

"Sounds to me like a couple of young gentlemen owe Mrs. Tillman a heartfelt apology and a new sound system."

A rock sinks in my stomach at the thought of how much a new sound system will run, how I'm ever going to scrape together enough to pay for it. I can barely conceive of how I'm going to apologize to Mrs. Tillman.

INCIDENT REPORT	INCIDENT NUMBER 875	REPORT TYPE: ☒ INITAL ☐ SUPPLEMENTAL

PRINCIPAL PURPOSE: Used to record information and details of criminal activity which may require investigative action. Used to provide information to the appropriate individuals within DoD organizations who ensure that proper legal and administrative action is taken.

ROUTINE USES: Information may be disclosed to local, county, state and federal law enforcement or investigatory authorities for investigation and possible criminal prosecution or civil court action. Information extracted from this form may be used in other related criminal and/or proceedings.

SECTIONS OR BLOCKS THAT DO NOT APPLY TO A REPORTED OFFENSE SHOULD BE LEFT BLANK

SECTION I. ADMINISTRATIVE

DATE RECD YYYY/MM/DD	TIME RECD (24 HOUR)	INCIDENT RECEIVED
1995/08/14	22:32	☒ In Person ☒ By Alarm ☐ By Telephone ☐ By Crime stop Call/911

SECTION II. COMPLAINANT

LAST NAME	FIRST	MIDDLE
Tillman	Marcia	Jane

ADDRESS	CITY	STATE	ZIP CODE
31 Sixth Street	Raven Brooks	MO	55555

OFFENSE COMPLAINANT

DATE OF INCIDENT YYYY/MM/DD	TIMES OF INCIDEN (24 HOUR)	OFFENSE STATUS
1995/08/10	18:02	☐ ATTEMPTED ☒ COMPLETED

OFFENSE DESCRIPTION

2 minors, age 12, pulled a prank resulting in damage to intercom/audio system of Tillman's Natural Grocer. Value of system estimated to be $5,000. No charges to be pressed, provided parents of perpetrators replace system.

SECTION III. PERPETRATOR

LAST NAME	FIRST	MIDDLE	ADDRESS	CITY	STATE	ZIP CODE	MINOR
Peterson	Aaron	James	910 Friendly Court	Raven Brooks	MO	55555	☒
Roth	Nicholas	Michael	909 Friendly Court	Raven Brooks	MO	55555	☒

I look at Aaron, but he won't meet my gaze.

Our parents arrive at the same time, and this is how they finally meet—with Officer Keith between them, explaining that they owe Mrs. Tillman $5,000 for new speakers, describing the prank in enough detail to take all the magic out of it that it might have held after the seriousness of our offense had passed.

Mom and Mrs. Peterson catch each other staring a couple of times, I notice, and in those moments, they almost look like the same woman—strong and tired and angry, and not altogether surprised. Dad stands behind my mom, arms folded tight across his chest. Mr. Peterson stands beside Aaron, and this is the first time today I actually see fear in Aaron's eyes.

I want to say goodbye to Aaron, but something tells me this would be the worst thing to do right now. I immediately regret not trying once we get in the car, though, because the first thing out of Mom's mouth is:

"Well, I hope you had fun with your friend, because that's the last you're going to see of him."

"Mom! That's not fair!"

"You want to talk about fair? Let's talk about what my signing bonus is going to buy, shall we? Do you suppose it's a new washing machine?"

"No," I mutter, rubbing the bruise on my hand where the kindergartner bit me.

"Are we going to get cable so you can watch all those ridiculous movies you've been begging me to see?"

I don't answer.

"No? Oh, that's right. We're going to be buying Little Miss Namaste a new sound system so she can sell more eighty-dollar salt crystals to morons who can't see how pretentious—!"

"Lu," Dad says quietly, and she calms down immediately, not that she should.

Not only did I cause Mom to have to give money to a person who looks down on people like us, but I have no idea when I'm going to be able to hang out with Aaron again.

Tonight was supposed to be epic. I've never laughed so hard as when we were recording those farts for the synthesizer that night at his house. Now I can hardly remember why we thought this would be such a good idea.

I have never felt worse. Not after my grandma died. Not after that time I ate expired SpaghettiOs and thought I'd die of food poisoning. Not after we had to leave my favorite town, where I managed by some miracle to blend in. Nothing feels worse than being driven home with your parents explaining to you that you've disappointed them.

Nothing feels this bad.

Except being forbidden to hang out with the one person you've met in your entire life who maybe—just *maybe*—knows what it's like to be utterly alone and not okay with it.

That feels worst of all.

CHAPTER 13

After a week at home with no TV, no games, no dessert, and no outside contact, I've grown feral. I keep my shades shut in my room, and on the rare occasion I venture out for meals, the light hurts my eyes. I've showered twice. I've left the protest state of punishment and just given up on basically everything, which I think is what finally wears Dad down. He has to get some work done this weekend, and watching me sulk around the house is making him edgy.

Still, I almost fight him on it because there's pretty much nothing more embarrassing than when your parents try to make friends for you. Except when your dad calls it a "playdate."

"Dad, answer me seriously. Do you know how old I am?"

"I didn't mean an *actual* playdate." Dad's hovering over an early proof of tomorrow's newspaper, a red pencil behind his ear and another in his shirt pocket.

"Because I've got this case of the sniffles I can't kick, and you know how grumpy I get after naps."

"Okay, okay, Narf. You're a crusty old sage, a bona fide

adult with bona fide adult interests. You don't 'play' with friends. You . . ."

This new thought tugs him away from his proof. "What the heck *do* humans your age do?"

His eyes scan me for answers, none of them the right ones. Even Dad knows that, and he looks torn between quizzing me further or meeting his deadline.

"Just do me a favor," he says. "Go hang out with Miguel's kid. If you don't like him, I owe you a Twinkie."

A Twinkie. Dad means business. He's pondering the big, important stuff.

Which is why I up the ante.

"Two Twinkies," I say, and Dad lifts his eyebrow. "That's right, cowboy."

Now Dad knows I'm pondering the big life stuff, too, the kind that has me debating how much I'm willing to do to make friends in this place.

"You've got a deal," Dad says.

* * *

The Espositos live three blocks away, in the newer part of town, and I fight back the usual pangs of envy when I look at the neatly trimmed hedges and colorful flower beds and fresh paint jobs. The Espositos probably own their home. They can probably paint it any color they want or put as many holes in the walls as they need to. They could mount a basketball hoop or dig an in-ground pool in the backyard.

I wonder if it's too late to hate Enzo. He was cool at the Square, but maybe his dad was counting on him to take pity on me. Then he opens the door.

"Cool hat," he says, and he ruins everything because he's nice again.

Enzo pushes the door open and leads me through the living room to the kitchen. The house is big and new, but it doesn't have the fancy furniture and white carpets I was expecting. The sofa looks old and worn with its cracked leather, and the floors are covered in a warm, rose-colored tile that makes our voices echo when we talk.

Enzo tears open a bag of chips that we eat by the fistful.

"My dad said your dad made him laugh so hard once, he puked," he says.

I believe him. My dad makes everyone laugh like that.

"My dad said your dad went to school on a full ride," I say with my mouth full.

"Academic. He's gonna be pretty disappointed when he figures out I'm not as smart as him."

He laughs first, so I feel like I can, too. Enzo's that breed of nerd who can laugh at himself and skim by on mediocre grades. Something undefinable keeps him protected from embarrassment. I think it's a total lack of self-awareness.

Enzo also has more video games than I've even heard of. We sink into two beanbag chairs, boot up a tag-team brawling game, and trade insults the way you can when you're a pro basketball player or a dragon slayer or a half-human, half-bird ninja warrior because insults don't really matter anyway.

By the time we look up from the screen, I'm blinking from the light of the TV screen and burping nacho cheese.

"I don't think I'm going to be able to bend my thumbs tomorrow," I say when my character is KO'd. I lean back and rub my eyes.

"So who else have you met yet?" he asks. "I mean, it's practically impossible to meet anyone when school's out."

"Yeah," I agree. "Pretty much just you and Aaron."

Enzo keeps button-mashing and staring at the screen. He hasn't died yet. His warrior lizard is still throttling some cat man.

"Hmm," he says, and at first I think it's a distracted "Hmm," but then his lizard warrior dies, and he keeps staring at the screen without restarting the game, and now I think his "Hmm" had to do with Aaron.

"You don't like him, do you?" I ask, feeling weird bringing it up, but the thing is, I've made a whopping two friends in Raven Brooks, and it'd be great if they didn't hate each other.

And if Enzo really does have something against Aaron being not rich, then screw him and his impressive collection of video games.

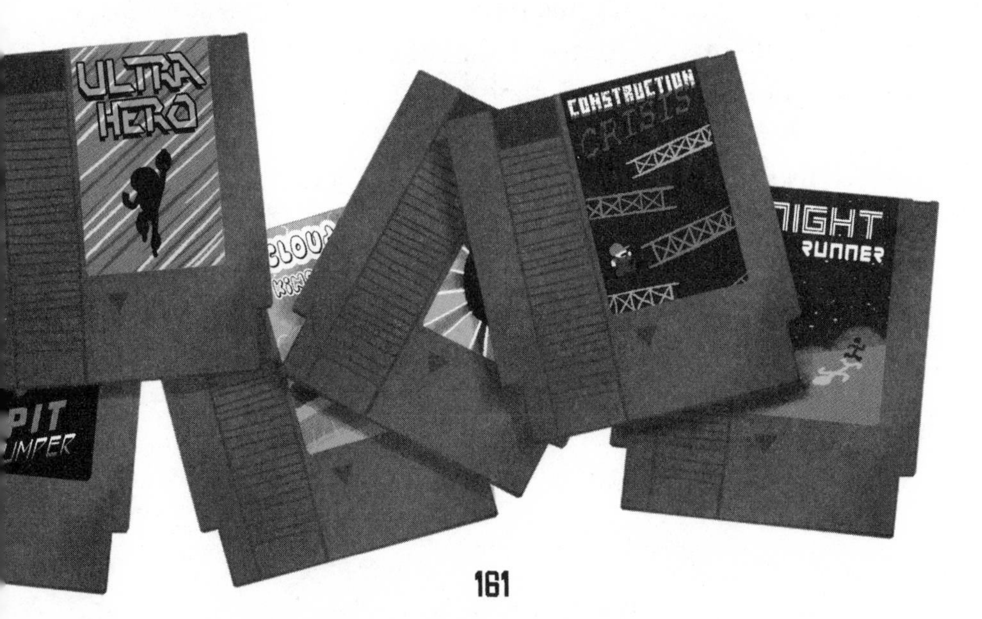

Enzo looks uncomfortable, and I take that as a good sign because if he is a shallow jerk, at least he feels bad about it. He sets his remote control down but keeps staring at the game's title track with the sound on mute.

"My little sister, Maritza, she's the same age as Mya," Enzo says. I didn't even know Enzo had a sister.

"She used to hang out a bunch with Mya and Lucy." He looks cautiously at me. "You know, the girl who . . ."

I nod, thinking back to the grainy newspaper photo of the Golden Apple Young Inventors Club. The third girl in the picture. The caption called her Maritza.

"So since I had to watch my sister and Aaron had to watch his sister, we used to hang out a lot together, too."

"Okay," I say, bracing for whatever bomb Enzo seems so reluctant to drop. So far, the only weird part of this story is the fact that Enzo's sister was the other girl in the picture, and she and Mya used to play with a girl who isn't alive anymore.

"We used to mess around at the construction site for the park. We were there all the time, and all the girls did was ask questions about how the rides worked. They were there so much, Aaron's dad even made up this Young Inventors Club for them. I thought it was pretty cool. But Aaron . . ."

I can feel the bomb dropping. It's like the air is getting heavier.

"I don't know," Enzo says. "It's like Aaron didn't want

them to be a part of the park, or around his dad at all. But it wasn't like he was jealous of us being with his dad. I just—don't think he liked his dad very much," Enzo says, but I can tell that's not quite what he means to say.

"Like he was afraid of him?" I ask, and it feels like a betrayal even wondering about what Aaron feels when he's not there to tell me if I'm full of it.

Enzo's eyes widen, though, so I know I've hit on something.

"After Lucy . . ." he says, then trails off. He takes a drink of soda absently before continuing again. "It just got weirder. I'd bring Maritza over to their house, but it was like Mya and Aaron didn't really want us around."

This is a turn I wasn't expecting. If Enzo was icing Aaron out because he didn't have money, why would *Aaron* be the one blowing *Enzo* off?

"It was what Mr. Peterson said to Maritza, though. That's what creeped me out the most."

My guts churn because I think I'm starting to understand. I swallow, but my throat still feels dry.

"We were all in the kitchen, but he stopped her in the hallway. She didn't tell me until after we got home. After that, we didn't hang out with Mya or Aaron anymore."

I ask, even though I don't really want to know.

"What did he say to her?"

Enzo looks straight at me for the first time that afternoon.

"He said, 'Did you see Lucy fly? She looked just like an angel.'"

It's like all the sound has left the room, and the only thing I can hear is the fan blowing in Enzo's tired game box. The lizard warrior cycles through his fight sequence over and over on the screen, but all the fight has left me. I'm not sure who to defend anymore—Aaron? Enzo? Mya?

What does *make a person bad, then?*

Being happy when bad things happen.

One thing I know, though. It's getting harder and harder to defend Mr. Peterson. At the least, he's just incapable of saying the right thing at the right time.

At the worst, there's something really wrong in the Peterson house.

CHAPTER 14

Technically, I'm not breaking the rules.

I say it to myself at least twenty times as I cut my way through the woods and edge past the overgrowth on my way to the Golden Apple factory.

I'm not going there to see Aaron. I don't even know for sure that he'll be there. I'm just trying to keep myself from going completely out of my mind with boredom during my last week of grounding. I mean, honestly, what do my parents expect of me? I can't ask Enzo to hang out every single second. And besides, he's in San Diego visiting his cousins. I mean, if you really think about it, I have no choice but to wander over to the factory where I've spent half of my summer. And if I happen to run into Aaron there, how is that my fault?

I can't even convince myself that this is a good idea, but who's to say my parents will even know I left the house? They're so busy trying to suck up to the important people in town—people like Miguel, and the Park family who do all that fund-raising for the children's hospital, and the city comptroller, whatever that is—they won't notice if I leave for a few hours while they're out schmoozing.

They're out schmoozing to make people forget you trashed Mrs. Tillman's audio system.

"I know, okay?" I say loud enough to startle some birds from the trees ahead. I'm already at the factory, though, and it would be stupid to turn around and go back home before I've even had a look inside. If Aaron is there, we've got some things to talk about. And by talk, I mean punch. I've been at the window with my flashlight every night, but he hasn't so much as opened his blinds since the prank debacle.

But the place is empty. Even the rats appear to have taken off.

"I know what you mean," I say to the memory of the rats. It feels like a betrayal being here. This is Aaron's place, not mine. He shared it with me, and now he's not even here to enjoy it. He's sitting at home, thinking about what he's done the way I'm supposed to be sitting at home thinking about what I've done. I'm still mad at him, but I wouldn't feel this bad if I didn't feel guilty, too.

I take a quick ride on the conveyor belt before I grow tired of that and fiddle with a few of the remaining locks we haven't breached yet. When that gets old, I decide to catch a movie in the Office. It takes me a little longer to pick the locks than it takes Aaron, but I get them eventually, and using the flashlight to guide me, I dig around in the filing cabinet and locate an unopened bag of sour-cream-and-onion chips and one last can of soda. I feel a pang of remorse popping the tab on the can, but I tell myself I'll replace it before Aaron has a chance to notice it's missing. Then, at the very back of the filing cabinet, I find an unexpected treasure—a VHS tape with writing on the spine I recognize as Aaron's.

"No way. *Tooth 3*!"

By far the best installment of the Tooth franchise, it's a miracle Aaron managed to capture it on tape. The utter genius of the movie—a psycho mutant with a single long tooth terrorizes a group of "innocent" popular kids—was clearly lost on audiences and never made it past the third installment.

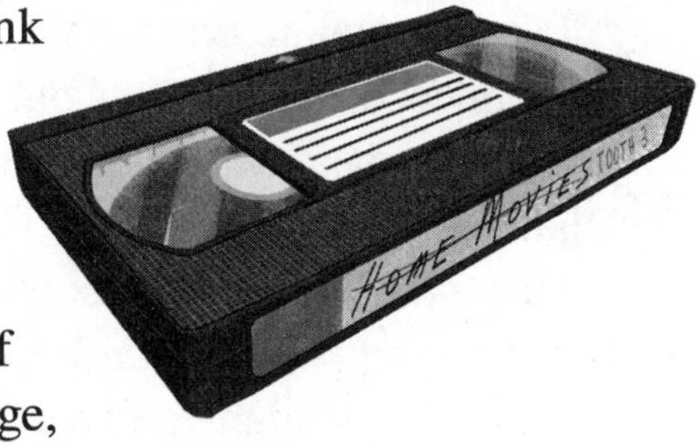

Aaron must have had a blank tape ready right when it came on TV. I park myself in front of the screen and munch my way through one and a half gory hours of dental carnage, pausing only to fast-forward through commercials I recognize from at least five years ago.

As my thumb slips from the fast-forward button on the remote, I catch myself watching a clip from a news highlight toward the end of the recording. A woman in a robin-egg-blue blazer smiles wide against a graphic of an enormous gold-and-red tent. “Don’t miss your first look at Raven Brooks’s very own all-season amusement park and entertainment venue—Golden Apple Amusement Park! Your exclusive sneak peek from Globe Five at ten o’clock.”

Suddenly, I’ve lost any joy for watching Smiley chomp his murderous tooth through unsuspecting teenagers. I don’t just feel bad about what I’ve done to Mrs. Tillman’s store. I feel sick. Maybe it’s the sour cream and onion, or the smell of the Golden Apple factory that I’ve never really noticed before. Maybe it’s the fumes or the mold. I bet this place is filled with lead paint.

But I’m pretty sure it’s the guilt.

I set the remote down and stand to shut off the VCR, but all at once, the movie cuts out as the credits begin to scroll. Static fills the screen, and in a single blink, I’m looking at Diane Peterson. She’s in a flowing dress and her hair is longer than it is now. It’s scooped into a loose bun, and her feet are wrapped in what look like leather straps. Her legs are long and straight, and she bends to the side with an ease that travels to her face. She smiles lightly, bends the other way, then kicks her leg high, turning and drifting from one side of the room to the other. There’s no music. The only sound is the padding of leather as it hits the floor she’s dancing on—a floor I realize is her living room floor. When

I look a little harder, I see the worn green sofa in the background, and on it sits a figure I know is Aaron only because of his posture. He's hunched forward, shoulders raised like he's waiting for something to creep up from behind. That's all I can make out, though. His face is blurred by distance.

"Here she is, ladies and gentlemen, the legendary Diane Peterson, Grace of Raven Brooks, Spirit of the Pines, Fairy of the Dance," whispers the cameraperson I immediately recognize as Mya.

"Oh, Mouse, you'll make my head swell," Mrs. Peterson says, but she doesn't stop dancing. In fact, she careens from one corner of the room to the other, lighter on her feet than before, buoyant on the cloud of praise Mya conjures from her tiny stature and tiny voice. Even at five, she had a better vocabulary than most people twice her age. She's like a tiny adult.

"Do the stag leap!" Mya prompts from behind the camera, and Mrs. Peterson obliges, catching some air before falling to the ground maybe a little ungracefully, but she's a true performer, never letting her audience—her adoring audience of two—see her flinch. And under the faint and enamored giggle of Mya at the camera's microphone, I can hear the breathless hum of Mrs. Peterson as she sings her own soundtrack.

I recognize the song—it's the same melody she was

humming that day in Aaron's room as she spread the sheets out for me on the bottom bunk of the bed and brought her mind to a happier time.

I hear a rustling off camera, and a man's voice booms with merriment as he hums the song, too.

Then Mr. Peterson walks into the frame. He's broad-shouldered and mustached like now, but he's younger, lighter. The burdens of his world haven't quite weighed him down yet.

"Mademoiselle, may I have this dance?" He bows formally to Mrs. Peterson and extends his hand. She takes it gingerly, maybe even tentatively, but when he twirls her once around, she smiles, and I can hear Mya giggle from behind the camera.

Mrs. Peterson continues to hum the melody breathlessly as Mr. Peterson whirls her across the room, his feet unsure but his face glowing.

In the background, I see Aaron stand and search the bookshelf for something, then squat in front of a credenza, fiddling with something before returning to the couch.

A song fills the room, its melody restarting from where Mrs. Peterson paused in her humming. The instrumentals of the song lilt through the air, and Mrs. Peterson seems not to notice at first that she's suddenly dancing alone.

Mr. Peterson stands in the middle of the room, staring at the woman he had once held so adoringly. Now he looks somehow disappointed by what he sees. Then he turns to Aaron, seated once again on the couch.

"Why would you do that?"

"I—I didn't know."

Mr. Peterson takes a step closer to Aaron.

"You *did* know," he says, and though I can't see his face, I know his teeth are gritted. And though I can't see Aaron's face, I know it's frozen in fear.

"You *did* know, because you *always* know. You're *always* watching," Mr. Peterson says, and the camera begins to shake as Mya trembles under its weight.

Mr. Peterson takes a step back, turns to the credenza, and whips the cassette from the stereo before hurling it across the room. It breaks against the far wall, falling to the floor in pieces.

"Maybe you should go lie down for a bit, dear," Diane says, edging toward him the way someone might approach a rabid dog.

He stares at her, betrayed. His great shoulders fall, and he turns his head slowly back and forth.

"You don't understand at all."

"I do, darling. I do. It's just . . . I think maybe you need some rest—"

"You always say I need rest! Why do you always say I need rest? All I do is rest! I can't rest while my brain is—"

He moves his arms in wide circles around his head,

making Mrs. Peterson flinch. I can hear Mya's breath quicken behind the camera.

Mrs. Peterson struggles to find something to say. I can tell by the way her mouth moves up and down. But she comes up short, and instead, she clasps her hands in front of her chest and lets out a little laugh that sounds anything but amused.

"I understand," she says, and reaches a tentative hand to her husband's shoulder, but he swats it away and takes a step closer to her as she stiffens but stands otherwise still.

"You don't understand. You have *never* understood."

Mrs. Peterson doesn't say a word. Instead, she presses her lips together, and the tall, proud dancer who was there before wilts to a fraction of her height. Mr. Peterson turns and skulks off camera, a door slamming outside the frame.

Mya sniffles from behind the camera, and Mrs. Peterson puts her hand to her mouth and turns to the camera, shushing her daughter and crouching, her hair now obscuring half of the picture as she holds Mya. In its new position, the camera finally steadies its focus on the couch in the background, and the figure sitting in it. I'd almost forgotten Aaron was even in the room. He was so quiet.

He's still quiet, sitting there staring at his mom and his sister, the weight of the entire scene pushing down on his shoulders. But his face is slack, motionless.

Emotionless.

I'm not sure what I'm expecting to see from him in that moment. Maybe something similar to what I suspect I'm showing on my face right now—the realization that Mr. Peterson is completely off his nut.

But there's more. The fact that Mr. Peterson is out of his mind isn't exactly news. What *is* news is that he was nuts while he was building the Golden Apple Amusement Park.

And his whole family knew it.

It's hot outside even after the sun goes down, but I don't feel an ounce of warmth on the walk home. I feel each prick of pine needles that I brush against and each drop of moisture that forms in the humid air. Most of all, I feel an icy, bitter cold at the base of my spine, and it keeps me trembling for the rest of the night.

CHAPTER 15

Anyone who says they're not afraid of the dark is probably lying. Anyone who says they're not afraid of standing in an abandoned amusement park in the middle of the woods—in the dark—is *definitely* lying.

It's hard to tell where Golden Apple Amusement Park stops and the forest starts. The whole scene is a kind of mangled-theme-park-versus-tree showdown, with branches protruding from carousel animals and vines curling around the ruins of concession stands and prize booths. Enough moonlight splashes down on the clearing to keep me from tripping over structures, but my shirt keeps snagging on spokes and gears, the exposed insides of the machinery that ran this place.

No one's supposed to see that part, I think to myself.

People get uncomfortable when they realize all that's holding together their cars and appliances are gears and wires. One missing bolt, and the whole thing collapses, and that's assuming the engineering was sound in the first place.

That's assuming the engineer wasn't crazy.

I check my watch and see that I'm ten minutes early.

"What am I doing here?"

I say it aloud, so I'm forced to hear what a stupid idea this was. Am I seriously so desperate for a friend that I'm willing to sneak out in the middle of the night to meet Aaron just one day after the *last* time I snuck out of the house to go to the factory?

I pull the crumpled scrap of paper from my pocket and read it for the hundredth time.

G.A.A. PARK AT 11:00. DON'T TELL ANYONE.

"Who am I gonna tell?" I ask the note.

Each time I read the note, the pit in my stomach widens. There's so much I need to know, especially now that I've seen that video. I can only guess Aaron's ready to tell me everything, which is why he left the note in the trellis, but now that I'm here, waiting in the dark and the nighttime chill that's begun to creep in with the approach of fall, I'm suddenly less eager for answers.

I hold my flashlight to see where I'm going. My sweater keeps snagging on the leafless branches, and the more I think about it, the more annoyed I am with myself for showing up here. The guy goes dark on me for three weeks, and all of a sudden, I need to meet him in the one place he hates more than anything—the place I practically had to beg him to tell me about, and even then, I barely got anything out of him.

I'm not really mad, though. I'm scared. Scared like a little baby.

"Get a grip, Nicky," I tell myself.

The peeling paint of the prize booths and the skeleton of the Ferris wheel hanging overhead clash with the gleaming pictures those early newspaper features printed. Smiling parents and wide-eyed kids crowded the park on opening day. It's hard to believe this place was so alive three short years ago.

It's hard to believe how much can die in that amount of time.

My flashlight clicks and blinks, and I practically drop it, fumbling to recover it before it lands on a warped picnic table.

The batteries must be low.

"Oh, that's just fantastic." I've used it to read Aaron's stupid note so many times, I must have drained what little battery it had left.

A twig snaps somewhere behind me, and I whip around with my dying light, but all I can make out is a small square of forest. Some clouds have begun moving over the moon, and now even the bigger structures in the park are hard to see. Everything looks like dark blobs against a darker backdrop.

Another snap, and this time I think it's coming from one of the shapes in front of me, though I'm having a hard time determining distance.

"Aaron?" I try to call out, but my voice is hoarse.

Get it together. It's just a bunch of trees and metal.

But as I open my mouth to try and call out again, the squeal of rusted machinery tears through the air. Gears grind and crunch as they break away from their vines, and with a roar, the forest comes to life with the unmistakable sound of carousel music. The blob closest to me begins to take shape, and I see the rise and fall of glittering poles.

I grab my knees to keep them from buckling as the shock finally wears off.

"Seriously, Aaron?" I want so much to laugh it off, but I can't get my heart to stop racing.

"If you're trying to get me to pee my pants, it's not gonna happen, dude. I'm like a camel. One time I went almost two days before—"

There's someone sitting on one of the horses. At first I thought it was my imagination, but then the carousel revolved, and revolved again, and the outline is definitely a person. A person smaller than Aaron.

Just as I'm trying to decide whether to walk forward or

run in the opposite direction, the music that seemed to propel the carousel around begins to slow. The high-pitched organ notes lower to a groaning echo until the spinning animals find their stop, the metal crunching to a halt as the music gives out.

I take a step forward, then another, telling myself there's nothing to be afraid of because even the remotest possibility—that some kid is playing out here in the middle of the night—is not exactly a threat. Who's afraid of a little kid?

I am. Because there's no way there's actually a little kid out here playing by himself in the middle of an abandoned amusement park. I don't care how much you like carousels.

"Um, shouldn't you be, like, at home asleep? I mean, you could get hurt out here," I say, reasoning with the dark, and why can't I get my heart to stop thudding like that?

"I'm, uh, I'm not gonna rat you out or anything, but you could get in a ton of trouble," I say, and now I'm standing right in front of the carousel.

Nothing but silence answers me. I take a deep breath and step onto the carousel, slowly convincing myself it was Aaron after all. Besides, it's way too dark to be sure of anything I saw, and the trees and the shadows distort everything.

I take one step, then another, and with the third I run straight into a metal bunny, its haunches planted on the floor of the carousel as it rears up. Its eyes glint red under the dim moonlight.

From the corner of my eye, something moves, but I realize it's just the mirror at the center of the carousel.

The shadow I saw was myself. I didn't see a kid on the horse.

"You saw your own reflection."

I shake my head, grateful no one was there to see me talking to nothing. This town really has me losing it. Maybe there's nothing weird about Aaron or his family. They're just people who have stumbled into some really crummy luck. If any family should understand that, it's mine. And maybe all that bad made Mr. Peterson go a little nuts. And maybe Aaron doesn't feel like hanging out right now. Maybe he actually feels bad about the whole fart-synthesizer incident.

I've just about convinced myself that I've fabricated the entire bizarre story of Aaron, when I remember that the carousel didn't just turn itself on.

A metal grate shakes behind me, and I hear a small thud hit the ground, twigs and leaves crunching underneath pounding feet.

I'm chasing after the sound before I know what I'm doing. If this is Aaron, he's not going to get the satisfaction of seeing me run away like a scared toddler.

After my lungs start to burn, though, I slow to a stop and

realize I don't even know if I've been running in the right direction. I put my hands on my knees again, this time to quell the fire in my chest, and when I look up, I see the twisted tracks of a melted roller coaster reaching higher than the highest tree that surrounds it. Branches protrude through the rails and jut skyward, defiant against the fire that burned half the trees that once stood nearby. At the top of the track sits a single car, perched precariously on the rail but refusing to let go. I can barely make out the string of peeling golden apples painted across the car, grotesquely cheerful beside the mangled track.

I follow the track as it drops to its lowest dip, a height just above my head, and I squeeze my eyes tight against the image of the car that detached from its fellow cars, like a bead of water off the end of a cracking whip, tearing through the nearest circus tent and crashing into the trees.

They thought she landed on the ground somewhere. Wasn't that what someone had said in one of the news stories? *They finally figured out she was still in the tree.*

I walk slowly toward the tree line, stepping carefully through the overgrowth of vines and shrubs that have cropped out of the ash. I don't want to, but I look up. I can't help myself. I half expect to see a car painted with apples, wedged between a fork in the branches, a little girl quietly bunched up on its bench, seat belt still secured.

The guy who found her said she looked like she was sleeping. She looked so peaceful.

I hear crying.

I don't believe it at first. I've gotten myself all messed up over the note from Aaron, the stories about the park, the trouble I've gotten into . . . the trouble I'm going to get into when my parents find out I'm not in bed right now.

The crying isn't in my head, though. It's faint, but I hear it.

"Hey!" I call.

I'm starting to get tired. This night has been one mistake after the next, and I'm completely over it. All I want is my bed and a dreamless sleep for once.

"Hey! Either quit crying or tell me where you are. Otherwise, I'm out of here."

The crying stops.

I wait, but not even a sniffle wafts over the air.

"Good," I say, even though I don't really mean it because if I turn around and head home now, all I'm going to do is lie in bed and wonder what I heard and saw and why this entire night happened.

"Okay, last chance. Aaron, if it's you, screw you. I mean that. If it's not Aaron, whoever you are . . ." I struggle with what to say next. "It's okay if you're scared."

Because I'm scared, too. I've been scared from the second we moved to Raven Brooks, just like I'm scared every time we move. I'm afraid I won't know where to sit at lunch or what to wear. I'm afraid of saying something dumb or laughing at the wrong time or not laughing at the right time. I'm afraid I smell weird even after I take two showers because our houses always smell like other people and no matter how many air fresheners you plug in, it still seeps into your clothes. I'm afraid that if I do finally make a friend worth keeping, he'll decide *I'm* not worth keeping. Maybe some people are just too weird to have friends.

"What makes you think I'm scared?"

It's a girl's voice, and I feel dizzy because all I can think of is Lucy Yi. I look up in the tree, and for a second, I swear I see a little pink car, an arm dangling from the opening on the side.

I feel a hand close around my wrist.

I leap backward, jerking my arm away from the cold grasp of fingers that leave a fine scratch along my hand.

When I look into the small beam of silver light that creeps through the tree branches, I see the illuminated face of Aaron's sister.

"Mya, what the—? Why are you here?" I sputter.

"I left you a message," she says, looking betrayed, like I should have known it was her writing me a note and hiding it in the secret place only her brother should know about.

"Okaaaay," I say, trying to process Mya writing me to meet her in the middle of the night.

"It's Dad," she says, wasting no time. "He's getting worse."

My heart drops into my stomach. The note from last month, the golden apple bracelet. It was Mya who left them.

"Ever since . . ." She looks around, and we both look up at the roller coaster above us. Then she says, "He's getting worse. Way worse."

I rub my head, which has suddenly begun to pound. I wasn't sure the night could get any more bizarre, but Mya is proving me wrong.

"I know," I say, aware that's the understatement of the century. Mya isn't the one I was expecting to see tonight, but maybe she could still help me figure out what to do next. “Is Aaron okay? I saw some things—and heard some things—about your dad. If you guys aren’t safe, we can call the police—”

“No,” Mya says firmly. “Dad was in a lot of trouble before . . . with the other parks. If the police knew—”

“Mya, whatever happens to your dad, you and your mom and Aaron . . . you need to be safe.”

“Nicky, you’re not listening,” Mya pleads.

“I *am* listening, but . . .” I’m starting to get desperate, too. “I just don’t know what you want me to do!”

I’ve never understood what people meant when they described someone’s face as “falling.” It seemed like an impossible feat for all the muscles in someone’s cheeks and mouth and eyes to just slacken and sink. But that’s exactly what Mya’s face does now. Except her mouth doesn’t just slacken. It shuts. Tight.

And just like that, all the tension leaves her small frame, and she takes a step away from me.

“You’re the same as everyone else. You don’t understand, either, do you?” she says, and she must be right because I don’t even know what is so wrong about what I said to her. I’m still so confused over the Mrs. Tillman thing and the video and that night in Mr. Peterson’s study, but none of that matters now. It’s too late to erase what I said.

Mya backs away three more steps, turns, and disappears into the surrounding woods.

“Mya!” I call after her. This is the last place either of us should be wandering around alone at night, but I know it's no use. I can't even hear her footsteps anymore. If that's a shortcut home, I don't know it.

It takes me nearly an hour to make my way back to the trellis in my front yard. I climb the slats carefully, conscious of every rattle and creak the frame makes as my weight pushes it against the side of the house. Then I slide my window open, replace the screen, and secure the latch. I sit there on the window seat with my head against the glass, watching for any sign of movement in the house across the street, worried about whether Mya made it home safely.

I watch the house until my eyes ache and finally close.

That night, I have the dream again about the grocery store. Only this time, I'm sitting in the front of the cart, feet dangling from a hundred yards up. I'm in a tree, branches crisscrossed over my chest, pinning me to the basket. Below me, my parents are as small as ants, scattering over the ground with dozens of others who call my name.

But I can't answer. I can't say a word. And soon, I can't hear them at all.

* * *

When I wake up, my head is still pounding, and I have the feeling for just a moment that I never actually went to sleep at all. My shirt and boxers are plastered to my body, and the way my bones ache, I wonder if somehow I was running all night. Is there such a thing as sleep running?

Then I remember the night before—with Mya and the carousel and the endless walk home.

My tailbone screams out in pain, and I realize it's because I slept on the hard window seat, slumped against the glass, my breath clouding the pane.

Suddenly, a loud smack against the window launches me from my morning lull. I groan and wipe the fog from the glass to find the *Raven Brooks Banner* resting at the top of trellis. The paper boy, we've noticed, has a powerful but inaccurate throwing arm.

Usually the Raven Brooks news is full of local announcements (*Catch of the Day at Dan's: Chilean Sea Bass!*), celebrity sightings (*Local Tile Maker Takes Third Place in Poetry Competition!*), and tragedies (*Lost!: Lovely Border Collie Answers to the Name Noodle*).

This time, though, the news is graver than a lost dog. This is how I find out about the accident.

After a long time, Mom calls from the kitchen, "Narf, can you come out for a minute?"

I drag myself off the window seat and down the hallway. I slouch in a chair as my father sets down his editor's copy of the paper and my mom puts a plate of waffles in front of me.

She sits down and puts a hand on my forearm. "We've got something to tell you. It's going to be hard to hear."

I methodically pour syrup into every square of my waffle, avoiding the eye contact Mom is desperate to make with me while she creeps up on the news.

"The paper landed in the trellis this morning," I say, taking a bite of the waffle I don't even want. "I already read it."

"Oh!" Mom says, then looks at Dad like, *What now?*

"Do you want to talk about it?"

"No," I say.

"It's just that, I think we ought to talk about it," Dad tries.

"I'm good," I say.

"Honey, you don't need to be *good*," says Mom.

"I know."

Now it's Dad's turn to look at Mom. They're stuck again.

So am I, but I don't know how to tell them that Aaron's mom died last night and I haven't figured out how to cross the street to see if he's okay and I've felt like I'm going to puke ever since I read the front page.

"They're having a service on Saturday. Your dad and I are going to go. Do you want to come, too? Either way, it's okay."

No.

"Okay," I say.

CHAPTER 16

RAVEN BROOKS BANNER

Local Mother Dies in Tragic Accident

Wife of Troubled Theme Park Designer Dead in Apparent Car Accident on Rt. 47

Everyone brings food to a funeral. They treat it like it's some sort of party, with these stupid paper plates that are too small to hold anything and casseroles you dish out with other people's serving spoons.

"You can just return it whenever it's convenient. Don't even worry yourself over that now."

People say dumb things like that. Or *She looked so beautiful, didn't she?* Like no one thinks it's creepy that you'd put a nice dress and makeup on a dead person to make them look alive again. Or *It was a lovely service*. No, it wasn't. It was hot in there, and my tie is chafing my chin. And it wasn't lovely, it was sad. That's why people were crying.

"Nicky, don't you look handsome," Mrs. Tillman says, suddenly forgetting that she had a lawyer send a letter to my parents demanding payment for the damage the synthesizer caused her store's intercom.

"Thanks," I say, standing. "I'm going to get more food."

"Boys. I swear, if I ate like they did, I'd drop dead of a heart attack right here."

It was already quiet in the house, just lots of mumbling and sniffing. Now you could hear a squirrel fart.

"I'm sorry. I don't know what I was—"

"It's okay, Marcia. Just shhhh, let's go check on the kids."

In the kitchen, I open and close some cabinets just to look busy. I avoid teary gazes and mournful nods in my direction until everyone finally leaves and I'm alone to contemplate how I've never been alone in this room. Actually, I've rarely ever been alone anywhere in this house. It's like someone was always watching what I was doing: I'd go to open a door, and out would pop Mr. Peterson. I'd wander down a hallway I'd never seen, and here Aaron would come, pulling me away toward his room or the kitchen. Even Mya seemed to linger on me. In fact, the only one who never seemed to pay me much mind was Diane Peterson.

Mom and Diane are actually a lot alike. *Were* a lot alike. Mom laughs at jokes Dad calls low-class, and she gets a headache when she drinks red wine. She likes cats and hates birds, and even though she says she likes dogs, I think she just says that so people don't think she's some kind of monster. Diane was the same way. But then she would drift, her thoughts wandering the way my grandma warned me not to let mine. She'd reminisce about the way Raven Brooks used to be, how welcoming and kind. She'd talk about neighbors who used to live there, and ones who still did but didn't come around anymore. She'd talk about the trips their family took to London and Berlin and Tokyo, invited by theme parks seeking Mr. Peterson's expert eye.

We wanted a quieter life, though, Diane said once, then smiled ruefully, and I know she was remembering how the aftermath of Lucy Yi's death was anything but quiet.

Out the kitchen window, I see Mom and Dad huddled close to each other in the backyard, peering over their shoulders to make sure no one is around. They're probably saying something inappropriate, something they'd scold me for saying. Or maybe they're just trying to figure out how someone could be here one day, on the road to the outlet mall thirty miles away to buy Aaron and Mya new jackets, and then . . . gone.

"Poor little thing. Imagine being ten years old and losing your mother. I didn't even see her at the funeral."

Mrs. Tillman appears in the kitchen doorway and stops talking when she sees me, then looks to the woman I think is Aaron's aunt.

"Lisa, this is little Nicky," she says. "Aaron's friend from across the street. His family moved in this summer."

"Nick," I say, and Mrs. Tillman's lips tighten.

"I'm going to find Aaron," I say. I don't mean to be rude. Mom would have pinched the back of my arm if she'd overheard, but I don't feel much like making other people feel better at the moment, and I'm pretty sure the only other person who's going to understand that is Aaron.

I walk upstairs and leave the low murmur of mourning under me. It's stuffy upstairs, but the air still feels lighter than it did down there, and I take a few breaths and head for the room at the end of the hall. Before I get there, I have to pass the master bedroom, though, and I'm surprised to see Mr. Peterson standing there, staring at the bed. It's made, and I wonder if he made it this morning because he knew people would be coming over after the funeral. Or maybe he hadn't slept in it at all.

He's turned a little to the side, which is why at first I think he's staring at the bed. It isn't until I get a little closer that I realize he's not looking at the bed at all. He's looking at the mirror beside the bed. Only, I don't think he's looking at himself. I think he's staring at something else he can see in the reflection. I try to see what he sees, but I'm too far away, still out of the range of the mirror and far enough down the hall so my reflection isn't there yet. I look at the wall beside me, but nothing seems out of the ordinary, nothing to be staring at the way he is—not aimlessly like he's daydreaming, but like he's *watching* something.

All of a sudden, I feel like I shouldn't be here, like I'm intruding even though I've spent almost as much time in this home as I have in my own. I want to run down the hall to Aaron's room, but whatever's going on with Mr. Peterson feels like something I shouldn't interrupt. If he didn't look so upset, I'd think he was praying. His face is all sweaty, and his lips are moving, but I can't hear him saying anything.

I turn around and head for the stairs. The kitchen doesn't sound so bad anymore, and I can wait for everyone there. Aaron probably wants to be alone anyway. Maybe Mya needs something to eat. And where *is* Mya anyway?

I'm almost to the first step when I hear Mr. Peterson make a kind of hiccupping sound.

"No," he whispers.

I lean back and try to see his face in the mirror, but I can't see anything from the stairs. I slink toward his room again, shoving aside the dread that's creeping in.

I stand where I did before, and now Mr. Peterson is holding his face like it hurts, except he looks like he's the one hurting it because he's pressing and squeezing so hard, his skin is turning pink and his eyes are bulging.

"No, please," he says, and it sounds like anguish, like begging. "Please just . . . *stop*!"

I open my mouth to say something. Is this what it looks like when someone has a stroke? Or an aneurysm? Or a meltdown? I turn toward the stairs, regretting more than ever saying whatever it was I said to anger Mya the other night. Their dad needs help—I need to flag someone down without disturbing him, but everyone's migrated out of the living room.

Then I hear a kind of squeal, and the first thing I think of is a mouse we found in the attic of the red house once, but the squeal turns into a hoarse cry, and I realize that Mr. Peterson is trying to scream.

I spin around to see what it is Mr. Peterson can't seem to *stop* seeing, and suddenly his face has gone slack, his hands limp and useless at his sides. His face is splotched red from where he squeezed it, but his eyes are half-closed, his gaze unfocused.

I'm about to bolt for the stairs to get help when a flash of white in the corner of my eye catches my attention. Aaron is there, standing at the end of the hall, his white shirt untucked, his tie perfectly in place. He's staring hard at me, like he's trying to see right through me, and for the first time ever, I have no idea what to say to him.

"I think your dad's . . ."

I want him to finish my sentence, but he just stares at me.

I try again. "I don't think he's . . . uh . . . himself."

Aaron doesn't smile, but his eyes squint a little. I expect him to at least be worried, but he just stands there.

Then he says, "Really? He seems perfectly fine to me."

I take a few steps closer to Aaron.

"Are . . . are *you* okay?"

He laughs a joyless laugh, his eyes no longer squinting. "Yeah. I'm on top of the world. Why do you ask?"

"I'm sorry . . . it's just, I don't really know what to say," I stumble through my explanation. He's obviously upset. How could he not be?

"It, uh, it was a nice service. I mean, you said some nice things," I mutter, and maybe this is why people say such stupid things after funerals. It's impossible to come up with the right words. Still, Aaron isn't making it very easy. We were hardly hanging out *before* his mom died. Now the accident. And there was that thing with . . .

"Do you know where Mya is?" I ask him, and Aaron goes silent. He's so still, I think maybe he's figured out how to turn himself to stone.

Finally, he says, "Why are you looking for Mya?"

I take another step closer because the glare from the window in the hallway is casting a weird shadow on his face.

"I guess I just want to make sure she's okay. I mean, as okay as she can be."

"Mya's . . ." he starts to say, then swallows, and now I'm close to panic. What if she never made it home the other night?

"If there's something going on . . . I mean, of course there's something going on. But if there was something going on, you know, before, you can tell me."

Aaron straightens his head, and his face is back in shadow. I don't want to go any closer to him, though.

"Trust me, Nicky," he says. "You don't want to hear it."

I hear a creak behind me, and the floorboard under me lifts the tiniest bit. I spin around to find Mr. Peterson standing a foot away. His face is still splotched pink from the pressure he applied to it.

I jump back before I can stop myself. It's just that I forgot he was even there.

"Tell everyone it's time to go home, Aaron," Mr. Peterson says, his voice flat and emotionless. Then he returns to his room, this time closing the door behind him.

When I turn back to Aaron, for the briefest second, I recognize the person looking back at me. His eyes are rimmed red, and his Adam's apple travels up and down his neck as he chokes something back.

But his voice is as emotionless as his dad's. "Time to go home."

I don't wait for him to tell me twice. It's not just a hint

anymore. He's telling me in no uncertain terms he's got enough going on to deal with any of the drama I bring. Maybe two kids with a bunch of missing pieces don't make each other whole—the perfect machine with all its parts in place. Maybe they just empty each other out more.

I'm halfway down the stairs before I hear him say, "And, Nicky . . . don't come back."

CHAPTER 17

I've held the gold-plated Golden Apple charm bracelet so many times, it's starting to leave a green tinge on my skin. It's like I'm waiting for it to break open and reveal its secret to me, to tell me what Mya wanted me to say that night. It would be easiest to just ask Mya, but predictably, I haven't seen her—or any of the Petersons—since the funeral. Not on the front lawn. Not in the windows. Mr. Peterson's car hasn't moved. I've walked across the street half a dozen times, but I chicken out every time I'm about to ring the doorbell. Either I'm too afraid Mr. Peterson will answer or I'm too embarrassed that Aaron might answer and be mad that I haven't done more to be there.

He told you not to come back.

That's the justification that stops my finger midair over the doorbell. But isn't that part of the messy process of grieving? My mom was a total wreck after my grandma died, and we knew for a while that she was coming to her end. Wouldn't it make sense that Aaron was all messed up, too, that he was just saying things he didn't mean? Wouldn't a real friend try harder to be there?

There's a fine line between trying harder and trying too hard, though.

None of this feels right—the leaving Aaron alone, the not being there for him, the sudden absence of any activity at all from across the street. Nobody seems in the least bit fazed that neither Aaron nor Mya have been seen outside the house for over two weeks.

"They're probably just spending time together as a family," said Mom when I brought her my concern.

"It's important to give them their space, Narf," Dad said.

I heard other excuses, too.

At the natural grocer: *Seclusion is probably the best thing for them right now.*

At the farmers' market: *That poor little girl must be devastated. She worshipped her mother.*

At the university while I waited for Mom: *I wouldn't even know what to say, honestly.*

It seems like everyone has a reason for avoiding the Petersons, now more than ever. I don't even care about all the unanswered questions at this point. I'd settle for an afternoon of Surviva bars and lockpicking.

But I'm not better than anyone else in town, because instead of flashing a note to Aaron's window or leaving something in his mailbox, I'm walking to a pep rally with Enzo.

As if Raven Brooks isn't weird enough, apparently they also have a different tradition around football than pretty much every other school I've attended in every other town we've lived in. They hold their first pep rally two weeks before school even starts.

"Why is everyone in such a hurry to go back to school?" I ask, moping even though Enzo actually seems excited.

"Dude, aren't you bored?" he says, walking faster than I want to.

Nope. "Bored" wouldn't be the word I'd use.

"I just don't get wanting to hang out on the football field and cheer for a bunch of jocks who would probably rather be punching people like me in the neck."

Enzo looks at me, and I swear to the Aliens, it's like it's never occurred to him that we're nerds.

"Why would they want to punch you in the neck?"

I have no idea what to say.

When we get to the high school, it's already teeming with kids way older than us.

"Tell me again why this isn't at *our* school," I say, a wave of nausea rolling through me. It's like the first day of school times a thousand. Everyone knows everyone. If Enzo leaves my side, even for a second, I'm sunk.

"Because technically, middle schoolers aren't supposed to be here."

"But all the middle schoolers come anyway?" I ask, so far not finding a single person who looks remotely close to twelve.

"Eventually, yeah," Enzo says, nudging me through a crowd of guys in backward Raven Brooks Ravens hats.

"I want a good seat," he says, and ushers me to the very first row of the metal bleachers.

Because nothing says cool like sitting in the first row.

"Can we maybe move back a little?" I plead, finding a perfectly invisible corner where I could easily make an exit once it's discovered we're LITERALLY THE ONLY MIDDLE SCHOOLERS at the high school pep rally.

"Shhh," he says. "It's starting."

Why I'd need to be quiet is a mystery. The cacophony that drowns us out even before the team hits the field is nothing compared to the clatter of the marching band that follows, all of them decked out in their purple jackets and plumed hats. Enzo stands and cups his hands over his mouth, giving an earsplitting hoot to the band.

"Aren't they great?" he says, beaming, and I can't understand any of it. Everyone's excited, but it makes no sense why Enzo is excited. Yeah, the band sounds great, and they have this synchronized wave thing that they do, but Enzo is looking like he's ready to crowd surf, and there's going to be no one there to catch him.

Except for the oboe player. Because she just blew a kiss at Enzo.

"Oh," I say.

"Trinity. Isn't she amazing?" he says, and I can't help but

smile at Enzo because I've seriously never seen anyone happier in my entire life. He's like one big, pumping red heart. Maybe only Trinity looks happier, with her glistening braces and waist-length braids and glitter brushed across her dark brown cheeks. I would have pushed my way to the front row, too.

After the game—not a game but more of a scrimmage since Raven Brooks is the only town to even be thinking about a pep rally yet—Enzo and Trinity and I grab cheeseburgers because the sushi place is already closed.

"Right? Who wouldn't pick sashimi over a greasy burger?" Trinity says, and if it's possible, I've found yet another oddball in Raven Brooks. She makes me like Enzo even more. I've never seen a person so blissfully unaware of his dorkiness, and someone else be so accepting of that.

Except I kind of have seen that with my parents. Weird.

After dinner, Enzo bumps his fist to my shoulder.

"I'm gonna walk Trinity home. You good?"

I nod, and I mean it. I actually am good.

That is, until I pass the natural grocer on my way home, and memories of farting the afternoon away on Surviva bars with Aaron fill my brain and make me feel guilty all over again.

The house is dark when I get home, and I find a note from Mom and Dad.

HOPE YOU HAD A GOOD TIME, NARF. WE'RE OUT BEING PARENTS.

I try to watch the Creepathon they're showing on TV, but I just can't get into it, not even when they feature the original *Tooth*. I realize that I'd held out the tiniest bit of hope that Aaron would make an appearance at the rally, even though I know that wouldn't have been his scene even before his mom's accident.

In bed, I stare at the ceiling and wonder why I've been so stuck in my head, so worried about what everyone else would think of what I'm doing or not doing. I've spent so much time trying to find a way to hide in every new town I start over in, I've practically forgotten that there are things people might actually think aren't repulsive.

"This is stupid," I say to the ceiling, and I get out of bed and grab a sheet of paper from my desk. In thick black marker, I write:

I roll the flashlight from under my bed—fresh batteries lighting it up bright again—and flick it on and off a few times at my window. Then I take a pillow and prop it under the flashlight handle until it holds the sheet of paper against the pane. I watch the window across the street for so long, my eyes get dry and heavy, and eventually I make my way to my bed, this time ready for sleep. I leave the note there, though.

* * *

I wake up screaming. At least, I must have been screaming because that's the last thing I heard before I launched out of bed, my back soaked in sweat. My throat aches like I've been shouting. I stand up, ready to reassure my parents I'm okay, it was just another dream.

Just another wandering dream. There was something different about this one, though. Something very, very wrong.

I was in the grocery cart like always. I was high above the ground, but suddenly I wasn't. Once again, I was wandering the aisles looking for help—my mother, my grandmother, someone to take me away from this place I knew I shouldn't be. The aisles grew darker and darker until they weren't aisles at all anymore.

They were hallways. Guided by candlelight, I walked along the hallways as shadows danced on the walls. I came to a room—empty except for a greasy paper bag. When I looked inside, I saw old take-out containers, two roaches crawling in and out of the to-go boxes. I backed away from the bag, but instead of finding my way out, I fell deeper until I was crawling again through the dark. I was alone, and then I wasn't. I was on a chair, carrying me higher and higher above a sea of faceless bodies. I screamed for help, but nobody came. I pleaded to go home, but a voice crackled over the speaker I couldn't see.

You already are home, it said.

Then the seat tipped me into the grasping hands of the bodies below. I was falling. Falling.

Falling.

Then I woke up.

I open my door, but no one greets me in the hallway. My parents are fast asleep, my dad's toes twitching from under the covers. It's still nighttime.

I close my door again, cupping my raw throat because it's impossible that I hadn't made enough noise to wake them, isn't it?

I look to the window and find my note still pressed to the glass, my flashlight still propped behind it. As I creep closer to the window, though, I see that something is different from before. Aaron's white curtain is billowing lightly through his own open window.

No, not open. *Broken* window. And not just cracked like it was before.

A jagged hole in the corner lets in a gentle night breeze, a hole I'm positive wasn't there before I went to sleep. The curtain isn't the only thing fluttering against the broken window, either. A white sheet of notebook paper dances in between the curtain and the glass. I squint, trying to make out what's on the paper, but it's no use. I'm too far away.

Grabbing my flashlight, I pop the screen from my window as quietly as possible, though apparently not even an earthquake would rouse my parents from sleep, so I might as well break the glass.

Climbing the shaking trellis, I pad across my grass and the street to Aaron's yard, more afraid than ever because of that note. That broken window. Something is wrong.

Underneath his window, I watch the paper flap in the nighttime breeze, but I still can't make out what it says. It says something, though, that much I can see.

"This is nuts," I say to myself, but I know it's not. "He'll be fine," I say to myself, but I know he won't.

Still, what am I supposed to do? Climb the tree to get the note he clearly meant for me to see?

Yes, you're supposed to climb the tree. That's exactly what you're supposed to do.

I've already resolved to go back inside to grab my shoes so I can get a better foothold on the trunk. But then a gust of wind kicks up, rattling the leaves above me and dislodging the notebook paper from the jagged hole in the window, sending it sailing into the middle of the street.

I chase after it, stepping on its corner right before it floats into a sewer drain. Crouching slowly, I unfold the lined paper to see Aaron's handwriting.

The message is simple, but it would only be simple to me. It reads:

It might be enough to keep me away for good. He's telling me to, in a way he knows only I'll understand. It might be enough to forget all about Aaron Peterson and his sister and his mom and his dad and their sad, fraught lives. It might be enough, except for the broken window.

Except for the thick smear of dried blood that streaks a line across the notebook paper.

If it's possible that Aaron really does make bad things happen, it's equally possible that bad things can happen to Aaron, just like a bad thing happened to his mother. Just like something bad might be happening to Mya.